Constance, Across

Constance, Across

Richard Cumyn

QUATTRO BOOKS

The publication of *Constance, Across* has been generously supported by the Canada Council for the Arts and the Ontario Arts Council.

Canada Council for the Arts Conseil des Arts du Canada

ONTARIO ARTS COUNCIL
CONSEIL DES ARTS DE L'ONTARIO

Cover design: Diane Mascherin
Cover image: Suzanne Cumyn
Author's photo: Sharon Murphy
Typography: Grey Wolf Typography
Editor: Luciano Iacobelli

Library and Archives Canada Cataloguing in Publication

Cumyn, Richard
Constance across / Richard Cumyn.

Issued also in electronic format.
ISBN 978-1-926802-59-6

I. Title.

PS8555.U4894C65 2011 C813'.54 C2011-903979-6

Published by Quattro Books Inc.
89 Pinewood Avenue
Toronto, Ontario, M6C 2V2
www.quattrobooks.ca

Printed in Canada

For Sharon

… and to him the meaning of an episode was not inside like a kernel but outside, enveloping the tale which brought it out only as a glow brings out a haze, in the likeness of one of these misty halos that sometimes are made visible by the spectral illumination of moonshine.

– Joseph Conrad, *Heart of Darkness*

YOU'RE QUITE COMFORTABLE? The shade is adequate? Adnan won't begin to see diners drift up here until well after sunset. Let me know, please, should you begin to feel light-headed. I have not forgotten that initial shock of heat, the brutal sun. Even now I can't say I'm fully acclimated. Lahoris say they're immune to it, but I know better. I've seen the way they dance in the street the day the wet monsoon sweeps in.

We could move inside. No? Very well. As I said, I can't quite believe you're here. It's a long way to travel to enjoy a respite from Ottawa's interminable winter. It was good of you, nevertheless, to give me some advance warning of your arrival. A woman, even one you consider to be cold and unfeeling, requires some lead-time in order to make preparations for your stay. Don't pretend to deny it. You did think of me that way and probably still do. It was true, after all. I was. That way, I mean. I did damage when I was supposed to uphold a standard of care. You could say I'm all about reparation these days.

I am sorry about James. Truly. I wanted to tell you that, the day you came to the school looking for me. Before I left. All right: before I ran. Like a coward. That would have been exactly the way it looked to you. And now you're here. For what? Explanation? A father who has lost a son must need answers. You've come demanding such, and rightly so. No one has a more natural right to them. And who but a man of means such as yourself, Grant Lungren, our erstwhile angel, could so successfully track his quarry and corner her, all the way over on the other side of the world? You are correct, sir, it did take much more than money. It took outrage, it took righteous perseverance. To find the one responsible, of course. But for what exactly, Grant? For punishment? Was that your motivation? Did you come for revenge? Living well didn't cut it, I guess. Sorry, that was a low blow. I'm left wondering, though: how is the act of confronting me supposed to bring your son back?

Breathtaking, isn't it? The domes of the great mosque are almost too bright to look at directly this time of day. And beyond, the formidable fortress, Moghul stronghold. I have a theory about such battlements and their impenetrable walls, the armaments and those who establish them. It has to do with the inherent vulnerability of the male of the species. You men are terrified of life. Your biology puts you at a distinct disadvantage, evolutionarily speaking. Like most tall trees you are designed to fail. You'd rather not hear about that. Fair enough. Another time.

You must be puzzled. What has happened to turn a woman like me into – how to put it delicately – into the person sitting across the table from you on the scorching rooftop terrace of this restaurant in the Heera Mandi? In this most Indian, most Raj of all cities in Pakistan. You deserve to know that much, at least. Why, it's because of love, of course, the kind that makes a woman lose her head, jettison career and family, run away from her husband and board a long-range passenger jet. I was thinking just now, watching you wish me dead, that this is like a story out of Conrad or Lermontov. A man travels thousands of kilometers in pursuit of truth. He reaches an important station in his journey. But obstacles stand in his way: the craft he is supposed to pilot sits wrecked on the bottom of the river, the climate sucks the vitality from his pores, his foreignness renders him weak, impotent, and he'll never come close to penetrating the fickle heart of this infernal country. Would you like to understand everything about Pakistan? Visit for a week. Want to be left baffled? Stay a month.

I'll try to fill the void, gladly. Not that I can guarantee anything truly revelatory, but never underestimate the joy of conversation in which your interlocutor actually understands what you mean by "No, really, that's fine, thank you for your offer." I've been saving this up a fair while, I'll tell you. And so, for as long as you can stand to listen…Why, to make you understand, of course, both my reasons for coming here in the first place and the circumstances which have conspired to keep me here so long. It will take some time to lay it all out. Even then…

You must know, first off, how grateful Tom and I were when you helped him establish his company. The ways of chance are uncanny, are they not? That James should have been my student then, and that my husband, enjoying his inexplicable and thankfully brief foray into the world of self-employment, should have been contracted by you to build you a new kitchen. Have you any idea how long I waited for him to give us a new kitchen? Forever, sans fruition. I used to be so materialistic. And, forgive me, what a crass complaint for me to express, given what you and your wife have suffered. I'm sorry. I said that already, I know. It bears repeating.

Those jousting kites, do you see them off to the left? They make me think of Afzal Khan, the man I followed here. Did he teach your son? Ah, perhaps that was for the best. In any case, his mother told me a story when I arrived, about how Afzal as a boy cut his hands badly on his kite string, pulling it in hand-over-hand rather than lose the flyer after the line broke near the spool. Did you know that they glue crushed glass the entire length of it, a painstaking process, to try to sever their opponents' kite-strings? The hours it takes. Boys can be so dedicated, so zealously committed to destruction. Or, at best, deconstruction. I should know. How unprepared they are when life wheels on them with vengeful, balancing fury. Are you still furious, Grant? What can I give you except apology?

Isn't it hard to believe that this country stands on the brink of chaos? America has all but declared war on Islam, Pakistan's raison d'être. India would like nothing better than to bomb us into oblivion. The Taliban are poised to regain control in the north. The place is a veritable powder keg. You must have had a difficult time actually getting in. No? I did. You no doubt flashed them your bank balance. But here, look around you: it's so peaceful in this cultural bubble. The Quarter of Forbidden Delight, I call it. Wait until after dark, when everything changes. I love it in daylight, before the men come hand-in-hand looking for what they can't get at home.

When I arrived, directed here to the Shahi Mohalla by the woman Afzal called his mother, the one who came to my aid was Adnan Mansoori, the owner of this fine establishment. He found me a job in a library, cataloguing English monographs. I never thought I'd become so adept at it, I, someone who couldn't keep her classroom files and lesson plans organized if her life depended on it. I've come to love the work, the concentration it demands, the serenity that descends, as all else, the incessant turmoil outside, recedes. Oh, I've watched the creeping havoc unleashed on this region by bin Laden and equally by Uncle Sam. What did the U.S. think when they invaded this part of the world? That a mere line drawn on a map was going to contain the Taliban? You think I'm siding with them, don't you, with al-Qaeda and its many hybrids. Think what you want. I came here to join the man I loved.

Ah, they have found us up here, finally. I recommend you drink a pot of hot, spiced tea with your curry. It seems counterintuitive, I know, but trust me, it works. You must sweat and you must replace your bodily fluids if you mean to survive here. Tom would thrive in this heat. My hot-tempered, wayward, simple man, though no longer mine. I've spent a long time trying to analyze everything that conspired to spin me off my axis and hurl me here. Do you believe we are the masters of our destiny, Grant? What I'm getting at is, do you accept even the slightest responsibility for the way things went wrong? I do and I mean to put it right.

Please, sit down, I'm not attacking you. The very last thing I want to do is undermine the legitimacy of your grief. Circumstance brought you and your son into our lives, just as chance brought Mr. Khan and me together. Parents cease to be the greatest influence on their children sooner than they think, and marriages die not from a single blow but unnumbered slights. All I can offer you now is my story, how I came to be here and what I left behind. It's the least I can do. You've come all this way for answers. Yes? Good. And for me. It will be a way of making sense of the unfathomable.

THE SIGHT OF him, how it flensed my soft tissue, tore muscle from bone, artery from organ. They hadn't removed his fingers or a hand, as he feared they might. Was amputation preferable to the pain he'd been made to suffer? Sometimes I wonder. Two guards dragged him supported between them out the rear door of that hellish jail and dumped him in the street.

Somehow we got him to his mother's flat, where he collapsed in a chair, looking up at us with the expression of a cowering dog when we lifted his head. He no longer recognized me. He shrank from my touch. His crime? He embarrassed the country of his birth. He had come to ours, that shining, cold, white nation of freedom and opportunity. He'd been privileged enough to teach in a fine Canadian school. And what did Afzal Khan do? He brought shame upon his native land, where so many hunger for just such an opportunity as he'd been given. His name appeared on a watch list. He was deemed undesirable. Something about a sum of money he sent while in Canada to a madrasa in Quetta. The details were never made clear to me. It's alleged to have been a training centre for militants. A bunch of little boys bobbing and swaying as they sit reading aloud from a book.

I wanted to take him to France or Germany for medical treatment.

"No," he said when he'd recovered enough to know where he was and remember what had happened to him. "I won't have it. This is my lot. I can tutor. I can beg. I am here, at least. I could be among the disappeared, as are so many. For that I must be thankful." He wouldn't look at me. His canes lay crossed beside him on the floor.

I was already in love with his people, the land, the food. Like his mother, Malika, I was growing fat on *parathas* alone. I'd long discarded my Western clothes. The day I waited for a street tailor to complete my first garment, I watched a sign painter create an entire movie billboard, first white-washing over the existing image, and then, working from a sheet of notes, producing a detailed and lifelike painting complete with captions in Arabic and English. The call to prayer interrupted his work. Normally he would have gone to the mosque. He must have been working to a deadline. He spread a thin reed mat on the ground beside the wall he was painting and made his observance, first doffing his sandals, rinsing his feet with water from a bottle, drying them, kneeling, bowing his head to touch the mat.

THE DAY EVERYTHING began to change, Afzal and I were on a city bus in Ottawa. It was a dark January morning after a night of freezing rain. He was standing two rows away from me and nearer the front of the vehicle. I couldn't take my eyes off him. I wasn't alone in that regard: he'd been turning heads since his arrival at the school in September. He looked like the leading man in that movie poster. He stood holding the handrail, his thick blue-black hair falling into his eyes. With his back to me he had the same slightly slumped attentiveness to the road as did the driver. Afzal ducked his head below the level of the bar, trying to look through one of the small, grimy, upper panes beside him. His hand moved tentatively from the rail towards the bell cord and back.

I was about to get up to tell him where we should exit, when the bus locked into a long skid. The back end of the car ahead of us veered left, correctively right, then glided left again with unreal silence out of the frame of the bus's windshield. He took an unsteady lunging step forward to maintain his balance. Someone nearer the front cried out, "Whoa!" There was a bang and I felt the shock of impact just before the bus stopped. I half stood in my seat trying to see what had happened. Gloved hands pawed at the glass, making blurry apertures in the condensation. People who had been content to sit beside each other in silence were now making unabashed exclamations of wonder, to seatmates, allies across the aisle, kindred commuters ahead and behind, and to the recipients of their phone calls.

His upper body was stiff and his head made quick birdlike movements. He turned and looked over his shoulder directly at me without giving any sign of having seen me. At the proper stimulus, it seemed, he would surely bolt. I raised my hand and was opening my mouth to say his name when he turned away.

The student across the aisle had her backpack greedily occupying the seat beside her. Seeing this, thinking of Afzal having to stand, and willing the bus either to move or open its doors to let us out, I almost said something angry to the girl, who sat listening to whatever was coming out of her ear-buds and trying to see out the window. To her I was not supposed to exist outside of the school building. I tried to recall her name. I felt I should know them even if they weren't taking my class.

Sirens sounded, the police arriving ahead of the ambulance and a rescue truck from the fire department. Flashing lights lit the left side of the bus. Some on that side had opened their windows the better to see the accident scene, and I welcomed the cold air on my face. Some passengers who tried to leave were sent back by a police officer who persuaded them it was safer to stay than to disembark into the jittery stream of traffic passing us on the left and threading between the two cars that had collided. The driver said we might also have to answer questions as witnesses to the accident. This brought derisive laughter from a man sitting behind me. "Witness to what?" he asked. "When was the last time this bus got washed? Nineteen seventy?"

WE WERE IN Lahore almost a week before two uniformed officers showed up at Afzal's parents' residence, a spacious, sparsely decorated house in the Gulberg suburb, and asked to see him. They demanded he hand over his passport and the letter outlining the terms of his employment in Canada, but he had only the former. He was to accompany them to the police station, said one. They gave him no time to pack a bag.

I told his parents that I was prepared to do whatever it took to get him released. I covered my head, was courteous and deferential and careful not to raise my voice. I had removed my wedding ring. In the worst of the heat I slept on a charpoy in the screened veranda at the back of the house. Each day, even when I felt sick from the heat, I went to the office of the District Commissioner and asked the same questions. Gradually the authorities paid me more notice. I told them what a fine teacher Afzal had been in Canada. There had to be a mistake. He had done nothing wrong.

His father said that a time would come when they would demand money of me. He said that I must not mention this myself, but wait until it was clear that the progress of Afzal's case would require an infusion of capital. A "goodwill payment," he called it.

One day Nabila revealed to me that she was not Afzal's mother.

"He calls me that," she said. "My husband and I raised him from the time he was in his early teens. He is my husband's son by another woman, one who lives in the Shahi Mohalla. Her name is Malika. She was a prostitute." Nabila said the word without sensationalizing it but with an edge of distaste in her voice. "She is a *naika* now. I don't know the English term. She manages the affairs of her daughters and nieces."

Nabila regarded Afzal and Malika the way one might consider a pair of mentally handicapped cousins. Tied by blood, one was obliged to acknowledge them in time of need. Love was another matter, one best left out of the equation. Nabila's regard for Afzal – I couldn't believe it wasn't love – was balanced by her exasperation: it was enough that he and his mother were socially embarrassing, a pair of *Kanjarian*, but now this arrest. All that he'd accomplished, his studies, his teaching career, the travel and work abroad, was essentially nullified. Clearly Nabila took credit for Afzal's success, but wanted nothing to do with me, his Canadian companion, at least not until he had cleared his name and extricated himself from prison. The fact that Afzal had been deported from Canada and arrested at her home seemed to perturb her more than did the fact that her husband had made another woman pregnant.

At that time a man could have up to four wives. Because prostitution was illegal – sexual relations outside of marriage was punishable by death – prostitutes referred to their clients as *shohar* or husband, each "marriage" lasting as long as was convenient to each party. Afzal's father's marriage to Malika endured a handful of years. Saleem was in his late twenties at the time and already married to Nabila, "his first and only true wife," she emphasized. One night he went to the Heera Mandi bazaar with school chums from his junior-college days at Edwards. It was meant to be a lark, a high-spirited, fraternal venting of hormonal steam. They could find some bootleg booze, watch some dancing girls perform in their *kothas* with the big doorways opened to the street during the allowable two hours, one each side of midnight, and get it all out of their system. What should have been at most a one-night fling became a passionate, complicated affair of the heart.

Nabila was home at the time with two young children. She was learning to love her husband, someone she had met for the first time on her wedding day. Their families had arranged everything. She had been studying dentistry in Karachi; Saleem was away in London, where he was earning a master's in public administration. The engagement had been relatively short. The betrothed couple spoke regularly on the phone during that time, watched homemade videos of each other at family gatherings, and warmed gradually to the notion that they were going to spend the rest of their lives together. They agreed that Lahore should be their home. It was the city where they had grown up, she in Gulberg and he in Defence, and though they had not known each other as children, their mothers were distant cousins.

Saleem loved Nabila, was proud of her beauty, her maternal nature and firm hand at running the household. That she had put aside her career was never a point of contention; she did not pine for what might have been. Saleem being a *sayeed,* she benefited, as did they all, from the status of that lineage connecting him to the Prophet. In all, counting one who had been stillborn, they had six children. The youngest two, in their teens, were still living at home when I spent my brief time living there.

RATHER THAN CALL his name, I got up and stood beside him. He was either in shock or as patient as a hunting cat. When I touched his shoulder he flinched. I could see the whole collision scene now through the front window.

He recognized my face, I could tell. He had to repeat my name three times before he could pronounce it with the sound of the letter T intact.

"Connie's fine, too," I said. "I don't think we'll have to wait too long."

"It is very bad," he said, blanching, his face lightening to the colour of untreated canvas. Beads of sweat popped out on his forehead and his hand slipped off the overhead bar. He sank in a controlled fashion, as much as someone blacking out can control his descent, onto the lap of the woman sitting closest to him. She moved her leg out of the way so that Afzal could perch on the corner of the seat. Blindly feeling about until he found it, he took hold of the handrail that ran along the top of the seat in front of him, and bent over until his head sank between his legs. I put my hand, gloved in soft supple black leather, on the back of his neck near the hairline. He needed a haircut. He'd been working such long hours, marking assignments, preparing lessons, slogging through the unpredictable English language, that he hadn't had time for a trim.

To have cool leather against the clammy skin of his neck – did it feel at all comforting? Could he feel the heat from my fingers? My bare fingers on his skin – he might well have regained his composure with the help of the soft touch of a woman's hand on his neck. This was my limit, not necessarily his. I'm no prude. Why, then, did the thought of touching him without the glove between my skin and his strike me as "going too far," as my mother would have put it? He wasn't a stranger. He was the man I wanted.

He straightened in his seat and stood, apologizing to the woman upon whose lap he'd sat. She told him not to think anything of it, asking if he was all right. Did he need someone to call 911? She opened her purse on her lap and removed her phone, waiting, hoping, I imagine, that the courtesy of offering to call would be enough.

Afzal looked at me and said thank you. I was about to say something dismissive – it's nothing, don't worry about it, you're not ill, that's all that matters – when the bus driver, returning from speaking with someone outside, announced that everyone had to leave. Another bus was on its way. A jagged piece of the body of one of the colliding cars had become lodged between the left front tire of the bus and its wheel well. "We're not going nowhere, folks. Sorry. Everybody off." We would not have to wait long for the next bus, he said. Fifteen, twenty minutes, tops.

A policeman was directing traffic around the accident scene. He let the northbound lane go by and then the southbound. We filed out with the other passengers. One by one we climbed over the snow bank and onto the sidewalk. We were in front of a branch of the public library. The high school was only a hundred meters away, on the other side of the road. A woman sat motionless in the driver's seat of one of the cars involved in the accident, her head caught between the neck support and the side window. It reminded me of newspaper shots of assassinated gangsters, their eyes open, mouths agape as if in mid-shout, upper bodies pinned back against the seat. Two rescue workers were trying to pry the driver-side door open with crowbars.

From the way the colliding cars sat, I couldn't tell which one had been travelling north and which south. They must have spun like bottles lying on their side. A man on a stretcher was being slid into the back of the ambulance. His hand made a gesture of nonchalance reinforcing something said, perhaps. "I feel fine, this is too much fuss, really, a cab will do me perfectly well." Glass lay strewn across both lanes, the tidily dull-edged cubes like raw gems spilled over black velvet.

I forced my eyes up and across to the dead woman again. Youngish, early thirties, no trauma apparent on her face though her hair was matted black with blood. Eyes closed as if asleep. I could feel Afzal shifting his weight from foot to foot beside me. Give me a minute here, I thought. I needed to see this. The wreck faced us square on, its windshield gone. No seatbelt held the victim upright, and it appeared that no airbag had inflated. A recent-model car. Was the safety device faulty? Had it been deployed in a previous accident and not replaced? I closed my eyes and saw the impact from the side, as if viewing the film of a test crash: the body, unrestrained projectile, flying up and over the steering wheel; the top of the head making contact with the glass; the windshield shattering but halting the body's forward motion; the inert bulk recoiling, inelegantly, to a twisted approximation of its former posture.

"How could she have been so…?" What? Stupid, careless, weak, indecisive, blind?

"It will be time for the bell," he said.

"I almost drove. Sometimes I don't put it on."

"Put it on?"

"The belt."

"Yes, it will soon ring."

He told me later that I spoke in a hushed monotone. He had to lean close to make out what I was saying. "Your outfit is freshly ironed, the last thing you want is to show up with your top wrinkled. So you leave the belt unfastened, thinking that it's only a five-minute drive. One second you're checking your face. Not even a moment to prepare. No warning. Did she – god. Did she have a clue what was coming? It's too awful."

By tacit agreement we began walking tentatively along the slippery sidewalk to a spot where we could cross the road safely. I glanced up at him. He thought by "awful" I meant the carnage. How could he know what I longed to escape? A sudden damp chill swept up my back. I lost my footing and fell into the snow bank.

He took my hands and pulled me to my feet.

"That could have been me."

"It was," he said.

He turned. I reached ahead to take hold of the belt at the back of his coat. I concentrated on his feet, stepping where he stepped, not looking up until we were at the crosswalk.

We parted company in the school's main lobby. Sometimes I think I want that moment again. I would be colder to him. I would not let him see so deeply into me. I would hardly look at him.

I REACHED MY classroom just as the bell sounded to mark the end of the brief homeroom period. "Hold it," I said, with less authority in my voice than usual, and the urgent egress halted at the doorway, clogging like a blocked drain. I needed to mark attendance; I could be late, lax, negligent, eccentric and domineering, but not to record attendance in homeroom every day was a serious and immediately noted breach of duty.

My first class of the morning knew they had a quiz to write as soon as they sat down, to test whether or not they had read the assigned chapters. As I walked across the front of the room, distributing papers at each row's first desk, some tried to persuade me to postpone the test. They had seen or heard about the car accident near the school. How could I make them take a test so soon after such a tragedy?

"Books away, please. Pass it back. This shouldn't take you longer than ten minutes; that is, if you actually did do the reading." They groaned, more for show than for real. An academic-stream class, they cared more about their marks than they wanted anyone to know. They knew me to be if not an entertaining teacher a consistent one, doing what I said I would, and by now they were conditioned to expect it.

With the class that came next, a smaller group, graduating seniors, I took up the homework questions I'd assigned. I was trying to get them to incorporate in their writing some of the classical rhetorical devices I'd been showing them. Most had put something down on paper. When I asked one young man, your son, as a matter of fact, to read an answer aloud he tried to make up something on the spot, going so far as to pretend that his answer flowed onto a second page. I could see from where I was standing at the front of the room that the page was covered with handwriting, work from a previous assignment. I decided as soon as he began to speak that I would override my instinct not to embarrass him.

"Would you mind reading that last part again, James? Just that last sentence."

He looked up, his face barely composed. His lips parted slightly, dryly.

"Go ahead."

He stammered something incoherent, barely audible, flipping backwards through the pages of his notebook.

"All right, that's fine. Forget it. Look up. I can understand you not being able to complete the work from time to time. All you had to do was tell me. You know I'm not one to bite your head off about that. It's the lying about it. This charade."

"I answered the question," he said, and despite his sullenness, bordering on petulance, he *had* given an answer, one that, had it been written, I would have awarded a high mark. He had answered the question pretty well. What was the big deal? Where lay the offence? He didn't know that this was hardly even about him.

"Everybody hand in your homework. Now. I'm going to mark it."

They protested. I hadn't given them any warning. It was in the rules, the student-teacher contract. At least give us time to finish!

"No. Now. It should have been done before you arrived. You have one minute to get it on my desk. I won't take it after that."

You can imagine the protest. I told them to be quiet and read for the rest of the period. Someone said sarcastically, "Way to go, James," and he looked both stricken and cocky, if that's at all possible. You have an aspect of that look about you now. I admit I let it get out of hand by making an example of him. I did what I was never supposed to, embarrass a student in front of his peers. I remember thinking he had it coming. He hadn't even tried to fake it. Technically he gave the answer I'd asked for. The balls of the kid! Smart, good-looking, knows it, too. They think they know everything, think they can take shortcuts everywhere. I knew I had to shove ego aside. What was I doing? What was this really proving? So what if he didn't write his answer down. He got it right and had even made a point I hadn't considered when I was drafting the questions.

The remainder of the period passed so slowly that at one point I promised myself that when this was over, this day, I would write my letter of resignation. It would mean a reduced pension. Tom's company was finally doing well. I could find something else to do: write freelance, edit books, work in a bookstore, go back to school and specialize in adult education. Travel. I'd always had the urge for going.

WHAT DID YOU think of the climb to get up here? Aren't those stairs something else? They remind me of the old romances I used to love, *The Thirty-Nine Steps* and *Kidnapped* and *The Prisoner of Zenda*. So narrow, spiraling upward into the darkness, each marble tread worn smooth, each step turning you a few degrees to the left, the passage as close as a tight closet, impinging on your sense of well-being. You rise through the cochlear passageway, which, as you'll recall, does not once open onto any of the intermediate floors. The day I arrived, the barefoot little boy I'd been following went ahead so quickly and soundlessly that it was as if I were doing this alone, that it had been my idea to meet Adnan to see what he might be able to do to help me free Afzal Khan and give me a place to live. It was fitting. I had come to this country with a companion who was now a shadow, unreachable behind bars. I might as well have come alone.

Are you upset by my portrayal of James? Is it embarrassing to know that one's offspring could be so dishonest? Pardon me? Other side of what, the story? There isn't one, is there. He's not available to give it, and if he were I'm not so sure he would contradict my account, Mr. Lungren, my portrait of him.

Do you know that Adnan is also a renowned photographer? He displays his portrayals of life in the Heera Mandi in museums, galleries and private collections around the world. Youngest son of a prostitute, he, like Afzal, grew up in the red-light district, and he too escaped, learning the skills of his art, teaching others, and becoming sought-after, especially by aspiring actresses who are always in need of high-quality headshots. He shook off the stigma attached to his origins and, with satisfying irony, returned to live in the very building where he had grown up. His portraits of prostitutes capture their dignity and sadness, the harsh hypocrisy governing their existence. If we're lucky, Adnan will grace us with his presence. He looks like Badger from *The Wind in the Willows*. You will see. He exudes threat, serenity and hospitality, all three in balance. At this very table in the shade of this same awning I told him everything.

"I can't go back. What if I never see him again?"

"You will," he assured me. "In the meantime you must live."

He had a friend, a librarian at the Punjab, the university where Afzal's father worked. Adnan would see what he could do to get me a clerical job there. Meanwhile there was a small apartment attached to the nightclub downstairs. He kept it for friends who came to visit, but his friends, he said, were all "sickeningly successful," with more money than they knew what to do with, and preferred to stay at the Pearl Continental. It was mine for as long as I needed it.

THE USUAL CERBERUS, the school secretary, had gone home for the day. I knocked on the open door. The principal, Kate Douglas, made me wait, long enough that I began to feel uncomfortable standing in the entrance, before she smiled, looked up from her computer screen and turned her head.

"I like that on you," she said, not specifying whether it was my sweater she referred to, a white cardigan my sons had given me for Christmas and which I thought I might never remove;

the necklace, a heart-shaped amethyst that was an heirloom from Tom's grandmother; or the new haircut, which was around-the-ears short, worryingly so because it was so different from my usual length and for some students the slightest variation in their teachers' appearance can affect everything negatively, from behaviour to attendance to achievement.

I thanked her. The compliment had been clearly a formality, something to check off Kate's list of automatic things to do to make us feel more comfortable with her as a manager and hence perform better. In a way it's not fair to characterize her this way. Hers is the one job I know I could not do even if I wanted to.

"What I wouldn't give to be able to dress down again, just one day a week. But when you're attending a working breakfast with the minister of education, meeting all day with parents who think you're singling out their children for torture, getting your ear chewed by a superintendent who thinks you could probably run your school on half the money you presently spend, and fending off store owners who want you to police your students while they're off school property, well, you have to look sharp, don't you? Sit."

The seat put my eyes just above the level of the desk. I almost stood again, but the low-slung chair was comfortable and I was tired. I did not relish getting on that city bus again. The roads were bare and only wet now after having been salted and sanded, and the temperature had been rising all day. It was the thought of not being able to see out the windows that made me apprehensive and wearier than I might normally have been. The early darkness didn't bother me. It was that outside the unwashed skin of the conveyance there were lights, visible stars perhaps, holiday ornaments still hanging on, prolonging the illusion of joy, and the thought of not being able to see these as I passed, to have them merely suggested as brief smudges, made me sad out of all proportion.

"I had a call today," said Kate, pulling me back from my mind drift, "from James Lungren's father. Not a happy camper. James is in your..." I knew what class it was. It was a classic ploy to draw me in.

"Twelve English, morning."

"Apparently James went home very upset after your class. He didn't return for any of his other classes."

"Ah, the irreparably wounded pride of the North American teen male. He thought he'd try bluffing me on his homework."

"Bluffing you. Tell me about it."

"My version of events, you mean." I knew how this worked. Kate would hear you, the outraged parent. Then she would speak separately with the boy, after which she'd hear what I had to say about what had happened. And then she would try to do what she was paid to do, which was make the unpleasantness disappear. She was good at it, I had to admit. Kate could have been a labour-management conciliator, she had that ability to listen patiently, make the parties feel that their concerns were ones she was willing to push all other work aside to hear, gently nudge opposing sides back on track and move them gradually towards the same middle point.

I recounted what I believed had happened. Yes, I'd had a chance to read through James's notebook, and no, he had not written answers to any of the homework questions.

"The answer he gave orally, it wasn't bad, you say. It covered the material."

"The kid can think on his feet, I grant him that."

"Did you ask him directly whether or not he had done the assignment?"

"Not in so many words, no. He knew that I knew."

"Did he?"

"Of course he did. I asked him to read his last sentence again out loud and he made a total botch of it. Look, I told him, and it extended to the whole class, not just him: it wasn't that he hadn't done the work."

"He had to have done something, thought about it after reading the material, formulated a response, in order to give the answer he did."

"He made it up on the spot. And he did it with this…I don't know…"

"Yes? Say it."

"This screw-you attitude."

"You felt he was giving you a personal slight. That's what you perceived?"

"Complete lack of respect. Deliberate insubordination."

"We're not the army, Constance. The days of Yes, Teacher, No, Teacher are thankfully long gone. Besides, this kind of thing never used to throw you."

"Maybe I should have let it throw me. Maybe I'd be a better teacher now if I had."

Kate leaned back in her chair and peered up at the ceiling. She wagged her head as if chiding a delinquent cherub floating up there.

"There's a connection, isn't there, between James' father and your husband? Or am I thinking of somebody else?"

"Grant Lungren lent Tom some money to start his business. That has no bearing on this matter."

"I'm glad to hear it."

"He helped us out at a difficult time. Tom had just left his job and was at loose ends, not really knowing what he wanted to do with his life and – you don't believe me, do you."

"Don't believe what?"

"That I acted impartially in the classroom. That my judgment wasn't clouded."

"I have every faith in your objectivity, Constance. I think that perhaps you overreacted with James, that's all."

"I didn't overreact."

She looked at me again, sternly this time. "I've scheduled a meeting for tomorrow afternoon after last period. Three thirty. You, me, James, his parents. I would like very much to make this go away."

"You should have been able to do that over the phone."

"Excuse me?"

"It's hardly a quandary. The child didn't do his homework and then he lied about it. He turned the pages of his notebook as he pretended to read his answer."

"Constance, I want you to listen to me very closely. We – the school, the students, the board of education, you, your colleagues – are not going to gain anything and will most certainly lose a great deal unless some sort of concession is made towards this boy."

"You want me to apologize."

Her mouth turned up slightly at the corners and she blinked once, slowly.

"This is unbelievable. I didn't strike the child. I didn't have sex with him. I pointed out a deficiency in his work and attitude."

"He feels ostracized from his peers, who are blaming him for being saddled with additional work. Punishing the whole bunch for the sins of one: not a very effective way to modify behaviour. That's a mistake a rookie makes, not somebody with two decades in."

"I'll meet them. I won't apologize."

"That's not what I wanted to hear."

"We'll talk about it tomorrow. I mean, really, Kate, where does it end?"

"Where does what end?"

"The erosion of a classroom teacher's autonomy. The ability to do one's job."

She drew a quick audible breath. She parted her lips as if to speak, but clamped them shut again. Bringing the nails of one hand together on the surface of the desk, scratching lightly, snagging an invisible mote, she said, "You're not going to win this. You come to that meeting tomorrow suitably contrite or don't come at all."

As if by prior arrangement the phone rang. Kate picked it up and as she did the look in her eye was one of dismissal. I struggled out of the chair. When I reached the stairwell leading to my classroom my knees began to quake.

I'VE BEEN ABLE to stay in touch with my sons by email. Each morning before work I check in. When I'm done I log off, empty the browser's cache, pick up my half-full coffee in its oversized paper cup, shoulder my purse and walk out of the cyber café. At first, in the harsh white light, I would have to stop, put on my dark glasses, blink rapidly, take them off and wipe my eyes with the end of my headscarf. I wore the same outfit every day until it practically fell apart, a white cotton *shalwar kameez* and thick, brown, rubber-soled sandals. In the street the traffic is always this congested and chaotic, the cars so puny and the donkey carts and bicycles and motorized rickshaws so flimsy and precarious that it has the feeling of a child's madcap game. You've seen by now how dangerous they can be. There are no sidewalks. Choking dust and car exhaust swirl everywhere. You can drink gourmet coffee while you shop online, but try finding a street sign. Even familiar landmarks grow strange. Scooters veer around you at the last second, the way skiers skirt slalom poles. I would suddenly have no idea which direction to go. In the distance I might spy the minaret of the mosque near Malika's apartment. At least it would look like the same one. I'd pull my *dupatta* tighter and draw it across my mouth. I would think about the snow finally having melted from the lawns back home. I conjured the smells of pungent spring: mud, drowned worms, salty dust, decayed vegetation, dog shit newly exposed and thawing. Somehow it all made the most glorious perfume after six months of cryonic suspension.

It would be eight in the morning and already the heat made me want to crawl into a tight corner of shade and lie down to die. The crowds bustled without hurrying, pushed in every direction, smiled for no reason, and regarded me with unguarded curiosity. They wanted my money. They touched my hair when it was exposed, held my hands, examined my fingers, tried to see inside my bag. Bearded men would gesture angrily, pointing me towards the narrow side-lanes. I saw only men in the street. So many beggars, so much desperate need. Filth lying everywhere. I have no doubt the rich would drive over the bodies of the poor with impunity if they stood in the way. Yet few have the lifeless, defeated, accusatory eyes I used to see aimed at me in the canyons of downtown Ottawa and Toronto. There it's possible to be simultaneously alive and dead. Here, the rare red traffic light seems to say "Relax" rather than "Stop." It's seductive, I will admit that.

AFZAL WAS SITTING near the spot in the bus where he'd been standing that morning, and when he saw me he smiled and indicated the empty seat beside him. I thought with some irony that this was the pleasantest moment of my day, sharing a seat on a crowded bus with a man who shared also my memory of the morning's trauma. I was too tired to say much. I might otherwise have said something about our still not being able to see out the windows. He'd recovered his composure and skin tone, a richly steeped tea replacing the ashy blotches. I asked him how his day had gone and he said that it had been satisfactory. His students were not particularly hard workers, but they had not made his job difficult. It was not like teaching school at his college in Lahore, where he was expected to be a strict disciplinarian, administering corporal punishment with a cane. He liked the fact that the Canadian school was clean and did not smell like garbage. He did not think that computers were good teaching tools. It made children lazy.

I asked him, gently, feeling that our brief intimacy of the morning allowed me to do so, if he would mind not talking any more about work. It had been a difficult day, I said, and I would appreciate the distraction. I rested my hand on his arm, lightly. This time my hand was bare. Conscious of the skin looking chapped, I withdrew it.

"Tell me about your family. Something like that. Tell me about where you come from."

"Most recently I come from Toronto." He had taken an intensive summer course at OISE to gain certification allowing him to teach in the province.

"You know what I mean. Tell me everything you love about your home."

"I miss about that place little upon little."

He retreated to a region of deep brooding, either locked in or out of his past. I wanted to know which. We did not speak for the rest of the bus ride until I stood to leave.

"My stop."

"Yes, I know."

"Goodbye, Afzal. See you tomorrow." He knew it was my stop. He'd noted that.

"Tomorrow. Goodbye."

He was observant, I decided, nothing more than that. But how many times had I taken the bus to work since September? Four? There was the time my car went into the shop for brake work. The time Tom's went in for servicing and he took mine to work. Once when the garage door malfunctioned, stranding both vehicles, Tom took an expensive cab ride while I walked to school. But that wasn't a bus trip, was it? So, only three times, counting today. Was it a language gap, then? Was he saying, "Yes, I know it is your stop," because the evidence indicated it? Why else would I be getting off the bus? Yes, I know, because you have just now told me so. The possibility that he had not been observing me seemed as unsettling as did the equally slight chance that he had. Why was I making more of this than common sense dictated? Why do we, suddenly awakened to the intersection of fantasy and possibility, magnify every iota suggesting the slightest connection? He was just a nice man. He was intensely private. He'd had a traumatic start to his day. Stop thinking about him, I told myself. He's not the answer to your problems.

I TRACKED DOWN Afzal's mother and explained who I was. Malika was skeptical at first, but I finally convinced her to show me where to go and how to deal with the functionaries populating the creaky, glacially slow bureaucracy. She taught me some Urdu phrases: "I am Canadian." "I speak only English." "Tell me what I want to know about the case of Afzal Khan." A torrent would flow in response and then someone would step forward to translate. There was always someone nearby eager to practice his English.

Almost a month had passed since I'd been granted a visitor's pass to the prison near Islamabad. Men and women simply vanished in this country. I'd gone to a bank, opened an account and transferred one of my registered savings plans there. So far I'd made two payments, thirty-five hundred American dollars and, a week later, sixty-five hundred, and still I was no closer to securing Afzal's release than on that first day we'd visited the district commissioner in charge of the case.

It was a shabby office filled with petitioners in the waiting room, some seated in chairs, most standing or squatting, some talking on cell phones, others making imploring gestures to the secretary, a self-important looking man seated at a small reception desk. Small boys came and went, with sometimes mournful, sometimes blank or happy looks on their faces. They delivered pieces of paper or fried snacks from the *wallas* in the street, and took orders for food, tea and lemonade. A policeman standing before the entrance at street-level appeared to be permanently attached to the DC's office, regulating the flow of petitioners in and out of the building, which may or may not have housed other offices. He checked people's documentation and credentials, listened as animated men and some older women related their tales of injustice as if he had the authority to rule upon their case. The initiated knew to follow his orders but to offer no more information than what he demanded, for they understood that his job was to find the slightest reason to turn them away.

I learned from Malika and these other veterans to adopt a manner of grave importance. Polite but reserved condescension took me the farthest at any given stage, as if this were one of my son Colin's video games and each time I arrived to play I began at the same point: this tall grim gatekeeper with his thick black mustache and compact machine-gun slung over his shoulder. Although he had seen me every day for the past twenty, he never indicated that he recognized me. If anything he grew pricklier each time he saw me. I learned to pull my *dupatta* farther down over my hair and across my face and neck. I avoided looking directly into the man's angry eyes. He hates me, I decided. Hates women, foreign women doubly so.

Most days I made it past the police officer, but then again most days I sat in the waiting room without being granted an audience with the DC. I learned to go in the morning, arriving just as the peon was opening the office. The first few times she came along with me, Malika grumbled and swore, for she rarely went to bed before three or four in the morning and she was used to sleeping until after noon. She also hated being near the cop, who she expected any moment was going to demand large sums of money in exchange for not arresting her.

"They know who I am and they know where I come from. A man like him, he might as well be a big *mullah*. Look at him, the sisterfucker. Don't you know he wants nothing better than to drag me by the hair and deposit me in jail alongside my son? Someone like him would never think of visiting the Heera Mandi during dancing hours. Now the DC and his cronies, that lot are another matter altogether. You know why nobody gets an audience with him before noon? He's taking Black Label and happiness from 2 a.m. onward. He's making policy decisions and having a fine time doing it. He wanted me a few years ago, but I spurned him. I told him I wasn't some Tibbi Gali *gashti* he could throw a few rupees at from time to time whenever he felt himself getting stiff in the pajamas. No, I told him, you have to take me away from this slum and set me up in a nice apartment and provide a healthy monthly stipend if you want access to this *kusi*. Cheap bastard. He hates me. I know this because he couldn't have me. Now he wants one of my daughters and I won't let him near her – she's too fine to waste on the likes of him, I'm saving her for a sheikh in Bahrain – and it's making him insane. Are things becoming perhaps clearer for you now, Connie? That fat water buffalo is making sure my son grows old and dies in jail before he lets him out."

YOU'VE MET MY sons. Colin, the younger of the two, was home watching TV in the living room when I came through the door. I was a little surprised to see him home, in fact, since he and his friend Bing were supposed to be working on a big science project together. I asked how it was progressing.

"Fine," he said. "Dr. Leung said he's going to look over what we've got so far to see if we're on the right track."

He set the table for supper. He wasn't at the point yet where he did this sort of thing unbidden, but when asked he did it cheerfully. He moves with fluid ease through life, I remember thinking as I watched him positioning place mats and napkins. He hesitated before deciding which sides the knives and spoons went on and which, the forks. It was his great talent to find, as water did, the way through.

When I asked where his brother was, all I got in reply was a shrug.

I put on a CD of cello music, poured a glass of red wine and began to chop. Our old collie stayed close, leaning into my leg as I stood at the counter. Afzal never thought much of dogs. He refused to believe we actually let one live in the house with us. I glanced at the clock. Tom would be pulling into the driveway soon. There was a time when his return could trigger relief, allowing me, finally, to feel increments of accomplishment, and I used to anticipate our reunion each day the way I might nurse a secret I longed to reveal to a confidant. I would hold it inside me the way I now took in the music, the wine, the calm of the house, and the pungent loyalty of the dog, momentarily frisky enough to jump up on our thinly upholstered old couch beneath the window.

When we first looked at the house it was the kitchen that convinced me we should buy it. This will be my space, I thought naïvely. Afzal taught me that privacy is a relative term. I was sceptical about being able to keep the kitchen's indoor-outdoor carpeting clean, but I liked its spaciousness, enough for a large round table, a sofa, and an old upright player piano. The piano was missing the roll that would have allowed it to make music on its own. My son Patrick learned how to play on it. We avoided it now that he'd lost interest in playing it. Sometimes it struck me as the deference paid someone who has lost a lover. In a way, we were like mourners who avoid speaking of certain things with the widowed party. Perhaps the old songs are no longer sung. If the deceased loved golf, to play a round without him now takes on an illicit aspect; the old television shows, impossible to enjoy except communally, are no longer alluring. Patrick had become so good, taking honours in music-festival competitions, mastering complex compositions – his favourite was Schubert – and beginning to develop a liking and the improvisational ear for jazz, that when he suddenly stopped playing the piano, at about the same age Colin was when I met Afzal, it really was as if something or someone in the house had died.

I looked at the dumb, scarred, dusty instrument, expecting it to begin playing on its own and, jangling like a ghostly set of Jacob Marley chains, shatter my late-day funk. I emptied the last of the bottle into my glass. If Tom didn't buy more plonk on his way home from work he'd be sulky to learn that I'd finished the merlot. He had beer in the downstairs fridge. Let him be annoyed, I thought. I'd needed this. I made the ugly piano disappear and replaced it with a tropical tree. Then I erased the sofa, torn, punched down, smelly dog's bed, and in its place ripped out the whole south wall, window and all, and put in glass doors opening into a greenhouse that had at its far end a glass gazebo with white wicker furniture and plump sturdy cushioning. It meant sacrificing the two apple trees. Who would miss those gnarled, skeletal, wormy crabs? Their spotted fruit ruined the lawn, rendering the soil so acidic that nothing else could grow there. I didn't realize then that I was reproducing Nabila's veranda in Gulberg.

I put rice in the steamer. Everything was sliced and chopped, ready to flip and dance in the wok. I loved the quick sizzling drama, the easy flourish like a magician's distracting hand gesture, with which I could create a meal. Until Patrick began to keep to himself, the four of us ate together. None of this "every man for himself" that was the rule in other households, as much as Tom and the boys might, at least for a little while, have enjoyed grazing for subsistence.

Tom called at five forty-five to say that he would be working through supper – take-out, eat-in – with his team. They were nailed to a deadline. The presentation for the client was first thing in the morning and they were not even close to being ready. It was going to be a late night. "Don't wait up for me," he said. He needn't have worried about that.

Patrick didn't call from wherever he was.

Bing Leung called for Colin just as I was preparing the wok with peanut oil. He wanted Colin to come over for pizza. His father had found some "stuff" they had to fix in their experiment. It's a science project, I felt like saying. You don't "fix" it. You take readings. You interpret the data. You communicate your findings. Tell him you're just about to sit down to eat.

"It's dark outside. How will you get there?"

"His dad's coming around to pick me up."

"Will he drive you home?"

"Can you?"

"All right. Call me when you're ready."

I turned off the wok, waited until I saw headlights shine through the sheers in the living-room window, called, "Not too late, you," in response to his "Bye, Mom," and listened for the car door opening and slamming shut. Cold air tumbled down the hallway to the kitchen. The rice was cooked. I turned the steamer off. I was no better than the boys when it came to eating alone. I found my staff directory and dialed Afzal's home number, but hung up after one ring. Appetite gone, I went downstairs into the basement, walked past Pat's room, went to the beer fridge and took out one of Tom's bocks. The first taste of beer always made me shudder and want to rinse out my mouth. All there was, it would have to do. Tom would drink two while he wound down in front of whatever late-night talk show was on. If I was lucky, by then I would be asleep.

I'd stopped loving my husband before I met Afzal Khan. Tom, as you must know, being his confidant, had an affair with a co-worker. It was short-lived and we saw a marriage counsellor for quite a while afterwards. It seemed to be getting better; at least I thought it was. Then Patrick began living apart from us. He was always a sensitive boy. He knew we were broken, Tom and I.

I carried the beer upstairs, picked up my briefcase and laid it on the kitchen table, a round wooden slab that had been Tom's father's poker table. It was as sturdy as an outcrop and sat at just the right height for writing upon by hand. I wiped some dried egg off the surface before taking out my marking. The radio blessed me with instrumental music that was rhythmic and understated.

I flipped through some student notebooks. If they had made the effort to write something down in answer to the questions, they got a checkmark and five marks added to their homework and class-participation evaluation, which was worth ten percent of the final grade. The conscientious ones put the effort in, even knowing that this five-mark check would translate into a minuscule percentage. The ones who were content with a middling grade saved their wind for the races that counted, the mid-term and final exams. They were working the system. Who could blame them, right, Grant? Why should they miss a sporting chance to gain the greatest reward from the least effort? I say throw out the entire grading system and start over. Throw out grades. And don't forget capitalism. And marriage, while we're being revolutionary.

THE WORK I was doing in the university library, cataloguing new monographs, was finicky, taking all my concentration, but I was getting better at it. I liked my supervisor, a man who was a bit high-strung with the others in the department but patient and cordial with me. He's been teaching me to read and write Arabic. My goal is to read the entire Qur'an in the original.

Contrary to what Afzal had said, he didn't have to resort to begging. A cousin got him a job keeping the accounts for a company that made leather clothing. He could sit most of the day while he worked. I didn't know what my public role with him was supposed to be. Every day he announced his debt to me as his liberator. I didn't know how to respond. There was no debt. I had chosen to be with him. I stayed on in Adnan's tiny guest room behind the bar, and most evenings before dark I walked to Malika's to see Afzal. We told no one we were lovers, though it soon became an open secret.

Though he could walk short distances using his canes, he wasn't going to improve without surgery and proper rehabilitation. I couldn't fully enjoy his body when he grimaced with every movement and looked at me with such gratitude. I confronted him with these thoughts, these doubts. Did he really need me there? What was my role to be, my active part in his life?

COLIN CALLED AT nine forty-five to say that he and Bing had finished what they were doing. I took my car keys off the hook, checked the stove to see that the burners were turned off, tested the back door to make sure it was locked, put on my boots and coat, and walked through to the garage.

So this is his private entrance, I thought, wondering if what Colin had said was true, that his brother brought girls down into his room this way. Oh, God, I thought. Did Tom ever get around to having 'the talk' with him? Too late now, surely, given what the boy had access to on the Internet. He could have seen every conceivable act depicted and still not know anything; he could be aware of only the barest rudiments of sex – physiognomy, technique, precaution, prevention, health – and yet intuit the finer, more complex rhythms of lovemaking. Knowing his nature, I assumed it was the latter. How did you handle the situation, you know, with James? Did you talk openly with him about these matters? Somehow I knew you were going to say that very thing, Grant.

I remember saying aloud, "Why are you punishing us this way? We tried. This is the arrangement we could live with," as if Patrick were in the car with me. I waited as the garage door rolled open and the car warmed up inside, my breath fogging the windshield and leading me to fiddle with the airflow and temperature settings. I turned on the radio. "Something," I urged the ether. "Send down sensible sounds to stuff this emptiness."

As I was turning off Riverside Drive and into the entrance to the condominium complex where the Leungs lived, I saw Afzal. I could hardly breathe. He was walking north away from me. I parked in a space reserved for visitors, got out of the car and, instead of going into the building, followed him, walking quickly enough that I was soon close, able to call his name and have him hear it.

He stopped, turning his head and shoulders towards the sound of my voice. As soon as I saw his face I realized I had nothing to say. Hello there. I love you. Nice night, isn't it? We deserve these milder temperatures and clear skies after the messy morning we had. Look at all the stars out tonight! So, out for a stroll?

"Constance. Good evening." Had he been practising saying my name? I like to think he had.

"I hope I didn't startle you."

"No. I am…" He looked uneasy.

"You don't have to say. I just…I saw you. I'm picking my son up at a friend's," I said, turning to indicate the building, "and didn't want to go in without saying hello. You've recovered from the morning?" He furrowed his brow. "The accident. On the bus."

"Yes, I… am forgetful about it. Slowly."

"Forgetting. Good. That's good. Me, when I'm upset like that I don't sleep."

"I am able to be asleep."

"Cold night for a walk." Stop. Leave the poor man alone.

"Yes."

"I wanted to say, also, that if you ever need to talk, about anything, I'm, well, here. It's a big transition. Coming to this country, I mean, and starting a job in a new school. It can't be easy."

"It cannot?"

"It must be difficult for you."

"Why must it be?"

"No, I don't mean that it has to be. Sorry, no, it's not a law here: all jobs must be difficult. Lord no. Just that I imagine that it has not been easy for you to make this change in your life."

"It has been made."

"I'll – I'm sorry, I should let you go." Obviously the last thing he wanted was to stand out in the cold talking to this intrusive blithering woman. On a dark sidewalk. Cars whizzing by. In his version of hell.

"Thank you," he said, nodding his head and turning.

"How far are you going? I could give you a lift."

"I am going only briefly a very small distance. I will see you tomorrow," he said in a tone that said everything was under control.

I'd run after him the way a breathless schoolgirl chases the crushing object of her affection. Clearly he didn't need my help. I wasn't even sure if he needed my friendship. Did he even like women? A man as beautiful as he was might have preferred his own gender. I couldn't help it. I liked it that he was so private, that he said, at least in English, what he meant.

IN THE CAR home I asked Colin for a progress report on the project. Bald, straight-on interrogation; I was too distracted for subtlety. After my awkward encounter with Afzal, it was as much to hear another voice in the car as to know the details of his and Bing's research.

"Fine," he said. Chalk one up for predictability.

"Do your findings appear to support your hypothesis?"

"Sort of."

"And the Nobel Prize in genetics continues to elude Colin Hardy."

"Mom."

"Just asking. I'm interested." Was it happening with him, too? Was he turning into a teenage werewolf already?

Colin activated the remote-control button clipped to the underside of the car's sun visor. As the garage door groaned open, the car's headlights caught a figure, half turned away and in motion towards the door that led from the inside of the garage into the house. Patrick shielded his eyes with his hand and moved aside to let the car in. A second figure passed from the garage into the house. The furtive way this girl moved reminded me of the racoons that sometimes got into our garbage cans. Stay, Pat, I prayed. Say hello. I haven't seen you all day. But by the time I'd brought the vehicle to a stop and closed the great articulated barrier behind it, he too was gone and the communicating door shut. Tom's parking space was empty. It was after eleven. The brief restorative peace of my evening alone was now a vapour.

I was closing the kitchen door that led downstairs to the basement and Patrick's room and, through a second door, out to the garage, when Colin said, "The kid mice are faster learning a maze, but they won't do anything if you don't give them food. The parents will keep trying for the food."

"They'll keep running through a new maze even if they don't get a reward at the end."

"Yeah. We can't figure that out. It's like, no payoff, I'm on strike. That's what the little ones are like. It's weird."

"What does Bing's dad say about it?"

"Nothing. He just smiles but won't tell us."

ONLY AS A child had I felt as ignorant and naïve as I did when I was new to Lahore, the difference being that when I was little I was encouraged to ask questions, and when I didn't know something it was explained to me. Those first few months with Malika and her children, waiting for Afzal's release, were frustrating, exasperating encounters during which, invariably when I tried to help, I only made matters worse. Noticing, for example, that the women wore jasmine blossoms in their hair, I brought some in from the garden.

"You waited too long," said Malika, bringing her nose close to my hair – a boy's cut, she scoffed, though in the interim it had grown out, into my eyes and down to my jaw line on either side. It dawned on me that women wore their hair long as much for practicality as vanity, for long hair could be held back off the forehead and up off the back of the neck in the heat. My jasmine, the motya flower, tucked behind an exposed ear, had apparently lost its fragrance.

"You must clip it before sunrise."

I stored the rule with others I was accumulating: cook root vegetables in an iron pot with the lid on, those that grow above ground, with the lid off. Let the cleaning women do their work. Stay out of their way. Let them change the bed linen, beat the rugs, spread the mats outside, where the day's vegetables, after being washed, peeled and cut, would be left in the sun to dry. Leave dirty dinner plates for the cleaners, who come in the morning. Tortoise eggs are rounder than those of a chicken, an embarrassing revelation after I returned proudly from the market one day. Test the skillet not with water but flour, which turns brown when the pan is the right temperature. The leaves of the Margosa will disinfect water. There were more varieties of mango than strains of the North American apple. The finest was the Langra, which I learned to identify. The best tasting take-home is found in Food Street.

A desperate efficiency is at work here. One day I watched ants in a martial line transporting large yellow crystals that turned out to be evaporated urine. It was yet another of my questions that brought teasing, counter-queries, double entendres. Men could relieve themselves anywhere. "Were you a bad girl, Connie? Were you hiding behind a bush and peeking at the boys? Tsk-tsk." Eat apricots to relieve bladder discomfort. Allow gypsies to operate close to the garbage dump. Wait. Be patient. Watch and learn. He will be out soon. They can't hold him forever.

I WOKE AT seven minutes past one by the red-eyed alarm clock's digital face, thinking that it had been the sound of Tom coming in that roused me. I waited, but the house was quiet. Was it Colin sleepwalking again? I got out of bed, opened the bedroom door, listened, went to the window, parted the curtains and looked out on the street below. A figure was walking away: female, young, long dark hair, jeans, a light-coloured bomber jacket, puffy, down-filled. I caught a glimpse of the girl from behind as she passed under a street lamp. She could have been coming from anywhere, going anywhere. No, she came from here. She was here in my house as I slept. I knew that and did nothing.

I lay awake for the next hour. I had a full day of teaching ahead with only one period off. I tried a visualization trick that had worked before. Picture yourself floating alone in a yellow inflatable life raft. It has a canopy to shade you from the hot sun. Warm tropical breezes caress your body. But it's not working. The raft shakes with violent tremor and begins moving erratically upon the water. I would never be rescued. I couldn't remember what I'd planned to cover in my first class of the day. The class after that, what was it? The answer eluded me. I almost phoned Afzal, thinking the sound of his voice would calm me.

Sleep came finally with the aid of a pill. As I felt myself falling, leaden, helpless, into the mattress and pillow, I pictured Colin and Bing's mice doggedly scurrying through unfamiliar mazes.

TOM CALLED WHILE I was still lying in bed, not long after the alarm went off at six. He'd stayed the night in the executive apartment his company leased near the office and where he kept toiletries and a change of clothes. I felt too punchy to be cool with him, especially since he sounded sorry and was trying hard to be solicitous, asking about my evening, telling as much as he thought I'd want to know about their preparations for the imminent pitch. Usually, so close to the event, he did not want to talk about it. So much was riding on this contract.

Crammed into a suit of fatigue that felt like cold, heavy, wet wool, I put on my dressing gown and went downstairs. I let the dog out to pee and watched through the window for her return to the back door. The dog liked to be present when her bowl was being filled with kibble, and so I waited until the animal, stiff, halting with arthritis, barked her one-note signal to be let in. She seemed hungrier than usual, thrusting her snout into the outpour from the large paper bag of food, scattering pieces around the floor. She would suck them up like a vacuum cleaner soon enough. Beside the sink was a cereal bowl with a spoon lying in it. Both had been rinsed. This could have been evidence of breakfast or a late-night snack. Patrick moved around the house so surreptitiously that I was beginning to think of him as a ghost or a living being occupying the same space as I did but in a parallel dimension. I knew I wouldn't see him before he left for school. I put slices of bacon into our heavy black iron frying pan, filled the kettle with water from a plastic container stored in the fridge, scooped ground coffee into a single-cup, paper-lined, cone-shaped filter that sat atop my mug, and went to the front door to retrieve the newspaper.

I roused Colin. After he had eaten his breakfast and I was assured that he was going to get to school on time, safely and with all the paraphernalia he required, I showered. I dressed in pants and a matching jacket that needed only minimal pressing, and decided to buy rather than pack a lunch. I rode the momentum just long enough to get out to the car, where, strapped in behind the wheel and shivering in the cold air blowing up from the vents as the engine struggled to heat up, I felt suddenly and utterly exhausted. If I hadn't been held tightly by the seat belt, I might have slid under the dashboard or toppled sideways into instant sleep. The garage door rolled open. I sat, drained of purpose, long enough for the car to become hot inside and for Patrick to open the basement door and peer into the garage.

Go now, I thought. Shift the thing at your useless right hand into reverse and let's get this day under way. I raised my hand to wave goodbye. The door into the house closed. Come out and I'll give you your first driving lesson, I wanted to say to him. Come out and join your family. Throw something at the windshield. Crawl into the back seat and crouch down, hiding, the way you used to when you were a little boy, in somebody else's car, somebody you wanted to be with and who was leaving; it saddened you to the point of inconsolable grief to see them go.

I had passed days far worse than this one was going to be and begun them in states far less prepared, far more scattered, dishevelled, depressed, premenstrual, hung-over or uncaring than I felt now. Then why couldn't I do anything? The weather was cold but clear, the driving uncomplicated by ice or snow, the roads bare white. No grubby bus to contend with. Clean windows. Things to see, look forward to, ignore if I chose.

I twisted the rear-view mirror so that I could see myself in it. Mascara was smeared at the outside corner of my left eye. Fix it, I said. Pull yourself together. No, I can't. I can't do anything until I think of the one thing, the thing to look forward to. Coming home at the end of the day. The peace of my kitchen. Yes, that's it. But my hand would still not move towards the gearshift or my right foot onto the brake pedal. Okay, how about this: seeing a single spark in the eyes of a student, that flash, that ah-ha! when she gets it. Still nothing moved. This is ridiculous. I'm probably filling the house with carbon monoxide. No, it's venting outside. Think. All right, this: the hope that I will come home and Patrick will be better. What do you mean, better? What's wrong with him? Identify. Clarify. Support. Conclude.

I was about to turn off the key, get out of the car, go upstairs, get out of my clothes, crawl back into bed and cover my head with the covers, when I thought of it. I was confused, so tired. I didn't analyze it, didn't ponder it lest I talk myself out of my motivation for doing it. It was enough to set me in motion.

Backing out of the garage and down the driveway, closing the garage door, stopping, looking right and left down the street, shifting into drive – had any series of simple actions ever been more of an accomplishment? My heart thrummed across the bars of my chest. Don't question it, I thought. It's real.

At the end of the street, where the previous day it had been icy enough to convince me to leave the car at home and take the bus, I signalled a right rather than my usual left turn. The traffic break was a good omen. The turn north onto Alta Vista and downhill was smooth, inevitable. I figured I would have just enough time to swing by his building, slow down in front of the bus stop where I thought he probably stood waiting each morning, stop the car, lower the passenger-side window, search the faces, find his, call his name, urge him to jump in, and speed away.

I was on Riverside Drive, with the Leungs' apartment building in sight, when I passed the empty bus-stop shelter. I turned into the semicircular lane leading to the main door of his low-rent high-rise. I stopped the car and let it idle in front of the door. No overhanging roof protected people from the elements as they went in and out, unlike the entrance to the Leungs' condo, which was elegantly sheltered by tinted glass. What if he didn't come out? What if he'd already left? I hadn't considered this.

When Afzal did appear, walking past my car on his way out to the road, I almost didn't believe it. He strode quickly, his briefcase bumping against his thigh. The raincoat he wore looked too thin to keep him warm. He wore a ridiculous quilted hunting cap, green and brown camouflage, peaked, with the earflaps down against the cold. His breath clouded, silvering his thick black moustache and eyebrows. I got out of the car and called his name. He looked bewildered.

"I thought you might want a ride."

He smiled and climbed in. I was amazed. I think I could have run all the way to school with him on my back. I could have torn the clothes off his body and made love to him, then and there.

"ONE DAY I said to myself that if I was released from the jail I would kill myself. It would accomplish the end of pain for me and the end of shame for my family."

It was a day off work. We sat dozing in the shaded courtyard of Malika's building, debating whether to take siesta out there or up in the veranda. The rains were coming, not soon enough. Afzal said, "Those were my greatest burdens. I cannot tell you which was the worse. But this much I can tell you: every day I am feeling better. Every day I wake up, I wash my body so that I am a clean man in the eyes of God, I pray, I do my work. I am a happy man. I try to be a good Muslim. I am glad that this happened to me in this way. The Almighty has said, Afzal Khan, this is how I wake you up to the real life of your possibility. Be a pure man."

A broken man. He couldn't be a pure Muslim and lie with a married woman, that much I knew. Who was he trying to kid? He'd been to hell, suffered torture, his penance, returned, and now contemplated his altered purpose in the time he had remaining. Even when he was inside me, he was more closed off than he'd been our two nights together in his apartment in Ottawa, or that day on the bus when I touched the nape of his neck, just where the hairline ended and the skin began, with the fingers of my gloved hand.

I DROPPED AFZAL off at the front entrance and drove around back to park. A group was smoking outside the tech entrance when I approached. I was struck by their hushed delivery, devoid of irony, as they took turns adding detail: the means and approximate time of death, the identity of the person who had discovered James's body, and the restrictions imposed by the police on traffic through this end of the school. In deference to me and to the rules, they took final drags on their cigarettes and butted them out on the pavement. These were the same slouching outsiders I would see waiting, almost daily, fidgeting and smirking in the main office, to receive correction at the hands of the vice-principal. Now they possessed the gravity of war correspondents or surgeons who could do nothing more to revive a patient. They looked far more grown up and composed than I was feeling, and it reminded me that this was their world, an immediate and violent reality no cop show could capture. I could go past the yellow tape because I was a teacher, one said, as if he and not I were the authority figure; everyone else had to use the front entrance. Increasingly shaky, feeling as if a rolling pin had been driven into my stomach, thankful for the company, I chose to walk with them back through the parking lot and along the sidewalk to the main door.

I had had students die over the years, those in my class at the time and those I had recently taught. Two girls had died in a bus crash in Turkey when they were visiting ancient sites. The school had organized the trip to that country and to Greece. A boy from Jamaica died when he contracted meningitis. Another two were in a car driven by a boy I always thought of as bad news; it had flipped onto its roof near Hog's Back Falls. There had been a little girl with cystic fibrosis who used to miss months at a time but from her hospital bed kept up with all the work. A young man had died in a ski accident. Had he been one of mine?

One of mine. The suggestion of proprietorship has always made me feel uneasy. The last thing I wanted to be was one of those teachers who became parental figures to their students, the overly familiar auntie they would return year after year to visit. Perhaps if I had shown more of this sense of possession, warmth, and the associated vulnerability, more of them would have come back to see me. But did I want that, necessarily?

Some might argue that I'd lasted this long in a young person's profession because I'd deliberately kept a distance, refusing to let anything become personal. I'd learned how to be emotionally detached, treating each task with the cool competence that, to an extent I was only now recognizing, had let me draw a distinction between what I taught and whom.

But this was too close. This shattered the barriers. The student I had reprimanded was dead, and all I could think was, Did I do it? Did I tip him over? Did he kill himself because of me?

I passed a pair of girls who were in my senior English class with James. They stood in front of two adjacent open lockers, hugging each other and crying. I stopped and looked back. I should say something, I thought, I should go back and be a comfort to them. I took a few steps towards them. They didn't look up. Their grief enclosed them as in a sphere. Words, those of an adult and especially mine, would bring them no solace, I knew that much. They would look up from their pitiful clutch and blame me. Of course they would. As do you, Grant. I turned and continued down the hallway to the staff room, where I hoped Afzal would be, but he wasn't there.

KATE DOUGLAS, WIRELESS microphone in hand, moved across the stage and down the aisles, reminding me of inspirational speakers who charged workshop participants thousands of dollars to hear vague platitudes, multi-step plans designed to empower them to change their lives. Step One: get used to living with thousands of dollars less.

Kate told us that the school would remain open the rest of the day but that classes would be cancelled. Classes would be cancelled the following day also. Grief counsellors would be available to speak with any of the students, should they need it, regardless of whether or not they knew James. It would take a few days for this to sink in, for the full impact of the death to be felt.

"I can't tell you why this happened. Maybe we'll never know. Your job today is to go home – wait until I've finished what I have to say, please, sit down – and give yourself time to think. Get in touch with your feelings about this. Allow yourself to feel something. It may be a quiet stream. It may be a turbulent river of emotion. Let it happen." A theatrical sob burbled from the back of the hall. "Ah, yes," said Kate, "very nice. Perhaps someone needs to see me later for sensitivity training." Tittering from that quarter reached a minor crescendo and died out.

We, the illustrious department heads, were seated on stage, as we did during graduation and commencement exercises. We were a mute choir backing the charismatic preacher, who was down there connecting with the congregation, a constituency that responded best to the illusion of openness. Kate's predecessor had been an administrator of the old school, a severe headmaster who would have made no public announcement in response to the death. Business as usual, he would have urged, back to class, nothing to see here, move along you young people. In a sense his was the more realistic of the two approaches. In the real world, if someone runs a hose from the exhaust pipe of his car in through the window and sits breathing the fumes until he passes to the next life, his neighbours are not assembled, informed, and prepped for emotional nursing. Maybe we should be, I remember musing. Then we'd be sitting and memorializing strangers so often we wouldn't have time to do anything else. Granted, this was a unique community, this school, responsible for the emotional growth and guided maturation of its inmates. Ours was a special place, separate from the larger world. We were nurturing the complete person here. We cared.

My stomach growled and I hoped no one heard. I wondered if my hunger and fatigue were the result of my late night or a reaction to this bit of administrative theatre. I had to pee. The day was shot. At least I'd have two days to catch up on my marking. The days passed too slowly when there were no classes to teach. It would be like being in prison lock-down: stay in your cell, do your work, look busy, keep your head low. I hoped I wouldn't get roped into doing grief counselling. I wasn't qualified to do that. I had no training in it. What if my students sought me out regardless of whether or not I was a designated counsellor? What would I say to them? Nothing, I would just listen. I was apt to lose composure, to cry harder than they did over James, and then what good would I be to them? The important thing was to keep working, not to let this throw me off. Despite the business connection between you and Tom, I really didn't know much about your son, whom I'd taught grade ten English two years earlier. He'd been a quiet, average, undistinguished student then, not much different from the way he'd been all that most-recent fall. You don't kill yourself because your teacher reprimanded you, not if you're in your right mind. Yes, I realize how hurtful it is to hear that, but I believe it, Grant. I did try to remember something about him, some clue, an instance of erratic behaviour that might have provided a warning.

My son Patrick was going to be James's present, permanent age in about a year. Why did I have that sudden thought? I didn't want to personalize this. We were a public school. Nowhere else but in a hospital emergency room are we thrown together in such an unfiltered way. Looking out at the darkened mass, as Kate worked her way into the audience, handing them the microphone and allowing them to ask questions or say what was on their minds, as members of the studio audience did on the daytime talk shows they watched, I considered the possibility that sitting out there could be the next serial killer, the next Governor General, the next crack addict, the next pope. A despondent student might take James's suicide as his cue to do the same. It happened that way sometimes, spread like an infectious disease. I suppose this was what Kate was trying to do that day, cauterize the wound, sterilize the area, eradicate the pathogen.

Leave me out of it, I thought, shifting uneasily in my seat. All I wanted was to get back in the car with Afzal and drive anywhere a long distance. Why had I worn those pants? I crossed my ankles to hide salt stains on the cuffs. How much longer? I really had to go to the bathroom. I tried to think about something else. The microphone was being passed from student to student along a row. They were all saying the same insipid things. I wanted to call out, Wrap this up! I was going to suffer a bladder infection. This is life, kiddies. Welcome to the ugly side. You are not responsible for every unbalanced person who crosses your path. You're not Holden Caulfield standing at the edge of the rye with your back to the yawning void. Put away your catcher's mitt. Believe me, it's not even close to being big enough.

The urgency in my bladder subsided. With guilt bordering on panic I realized that I had not thought about my own troubled son through any of this. What if…? But no, I would not let myself articulate the thought, even if it was already there, lodged, sending out its destructive pulse. If Patrick wanted to meet me halfway he was more than welcome. He needed help, but we couldn't do anything for him until he rejoined the family. It was demeaning for him to spend all his time down in the basement like some teenage Phantom of the Opera. The rare times now that he let his eyes meet mine, it was very much as if he were wearing a mask. Who was this child, spawn of my loins, stranger in my house? I couldn't get across to him. He stood on the other side of a deep canyon, mocking me.

AFTER LUNCH I walked along the main hall, past Kate's office and towards the north wing of the school, the one opposite mine and which I could see from the window of my classroom. Going up the stairs I met Gavin Fleck, you might have met him, another English teacher, and we chatted briefly about the suicide and its fallout. We agreed that, despite its shocking impact, neither of us had seen it coming. No one he had spoken with, teacher or student, had an inkling that this had been brewing. We didn't say James's name. How quickly had this become something that had happened not to him but to us. The boy had changed in a matter of a few hours from victim to perpetrator. How long, we wondered aloud, would it take us to recover from this? We mentioned similar, illustrative events. Recovery always took longer than expected. We would have to be tolerant of erratic behaviour in our students. The staff would have to be vigilant. We'd have to keep an eye on each other in the next month or so. This would be the time when people drank more, got sick more often, blew up at their children, hit their spouses. It was well documented in the literature. You did say you wanted to know everything, Grant.

"Kate should call a meeting and remind us of this."

"She's going to."

"Good."

"You're okay?"

"Yeah, sure. Shaken, certainly. You?"

"Oh, the same. You heard about the note?"

"No," I said, feeling panicked, barely keeping my rising dread in check. "I'm not surprised, though."

"That he left one?"

"Yes. It's a common – I imagine it's a strong urge in us. Actually, I have to watch that: making conclusions I can't support."

He met my eye briefly, looked away, then moved a step down towards me. "He mentioned you in the note. I assumed you knew."

"What did it say?"

"I don't know specifics."

Yes you do, I wanted to say. Tell me. Fleck was head of the union's local branch. Kate would have called him in, laid out how this was going to play out, in the press and possibly in the courts if the family sued. Your son had complicated matters by taking his life on school property. He had come in early, found some way into the automotive shop, opened the bay door, driven his car in and hooked up the exhaust hose. Somehow he had acquired a key, probably a master, although the shop teacher was known to be slack when it came to security. He had his favourites to whom he entrusted keys so that they could work on their vehicles after school and on weekends. James could have gotten a key from one of them.

What had he written about me? What was the worst he could have said? That I had humiliated him in class. That I had accused him of not doing the work and of lying about it. If every student, past and present, who'd had a grudge against me for a perceived injustice had committed suicide, the bodies would have filled a good-sized burial plot. Still, they hadn't. Only this one had. This boy about whom I knew so little. He must have been terribly troubled. How was I supposed to know this, to detect, to prevent? Let me have the moment back. I make that wish every day. Let me have that moment to live again and I'll handle it so differently. I'll ignore him, call on someone else. I'll listen to his answer and praise him for it. I'll acknowledge his quick thinking, make a joke of it, wink and let him know that I know.

KATE FOUND ME in my classroom. "I like what you've done with the place," she said, following her manager's handbook: *3.1.3. Dealing with Sticky Situations. Break the ice with a compliment or a humorous anecdote before communicating difficult information to an employee.*

I was not her employee. I was the one who stayed true to my calling.

She'd been allowed to make a photocopy of the letter that was found beside James on the seat of the car. The police kept the original. You've read it. You haven't? I find that surprising.

This will be revelatory, then. Here, let me find my copy. Ah, here it is. Kate sat at the teacher's desk while I continued to stand to read.

"Dear Mrs. H.,

"I'm addressing this to you because I think you're the one person most likely to understand. First of all, this has nothing to do with what happened in class, even though it was kind of dumb to make everybody pay for my laziness. You were right, I was trying to scam you. But you have to admit, it was a pretty impressive bit of improv. I guess what really hurt was knowing that you thought I didn't care about the work. Nothing could be less true. You, if you really want to know, are maybe one of only three teachers I actually wanted to impress in this fine institution. Not that I have to justify what I did or didn't do in class, but there are some things happening in my life that shall we say have been playing major havoc with my state of mind, not to mention my ability to study. I just want you to know that I'm sorry and I feel terrible about letting you down. About having let you down.

"Do you remember that assignment you got us to do, the one where we had to read that long article about the making of a Steinway piano? We had to go and research something like that and then write a similar kind of piece. I had the hardest time coming up with a subject. I mean, I loved reading about the grand piano, the fact that it took seven years to build, with so many steps and you had to wait for the wood to reach the right humidity and all these people were involved, with each one having a specific skill. It killed me not being able to find something equivalent. My mom was knitting this elaborate afghan and so I got her to tell me about all the steps that went into making it. You know this already, but for some reason I need to tell it to you again. Every square was different. It was all right, I guess. It got me interested in trying to do something like that myself. But what I really wanted to write about was everything that goes into making a person. Think about it, you've got genes and nutrition and environment, parenting styles and accidents and exposure to all the things that are bad for us. I know, it's way too much for one essay. For what it's worth, that's the stuff that gets me excited. Or used to.

"I don't know what I'm trying to say. I think it's close to the reason why I'm writing this to you, Mrs. Hardy. Constance. It feels a tad presumptuous to call you by your first name, but who cares at this point in the game? I mean, there's the shit about my dad lending your husband money and all that. Almost not even worth mentioning, except suddenly it gave me insight into who you were and what all was making you. who you were at school. Did you know that every year there's a line-up of losers trying to transfer out of your class? Probably old news. You do have something of a reputation, if it didn't already dawn on you. Mostly they've heard about how strict and demanding you are and they don't want to have to work hard. What they don't see, because they haven't had a chance to yet, is how much you care about the subject and the language. And also they can't see how unhappy you are. Maybe I've got a kind of radar for that sort of thing. I can spot somebody in crisis from like a hundred metres away. Not a temporarily sad type who's that way because she didn't get flowers on her anniversary. I mean someone who has to make a change in her life or it'll mean the end of her. I think you need to do that. I'm not sure what that change should be exactly. All I know is that it's dragging way out behind you. It's like you're fighting against whatever it is that's going to set you free. Or maybe I'm thinking about me.

"This is the fifth or maybe sixth draft I've done of this letter. The first couple were to whoever was going to find me. The next two were to my parents, then my dad specifically, and finally to you. My father is never going to change and I know I can't be the man he wants me to be. So I thought, who of all people I know would most likely get what I'm on about? Somebody who's got sons of her own. Somebody whose one son is going through some difficult crap of his own. Somebody whose husband – excuse my bluntness, but I pay attention – is too wrapped up in his reflection (a very favourable reflection, might I add) to see what our Somebody really needs. I like Mr. H., I do. That time he was putting in our new kitchen and he helped me with my programming assignment? Well, let's just say he could do no wrong for quite some time after that. And later, when he'd come over and Dad was helping him with financing and all that, it was clear why you were attracted to him in the first place.

"I can't believe I'm telling you all this. There are moments when I wish I could call you up or maybe meet for a late-night latte downtown, where we could talk and be completely unguarded. I so hate being guarded.

"I don't know what this is. Not a cry for help, not for me, in any case. What would you call it? You're the expert in textual analysis. Dad's favourite line is, let me set you straight on a few things. How much of a hoot is that! Well, to steal his thunder, let me set you straight on one thing, Constance, one big thing. Whatever's making you so down, you have to deal with it. Call this a lifeline thrown from the other side or call it a push, it's what I believe.

"I am sorry. Truly. For every little thing. I do think you're one of the good ones.

"James"

"UNDER THE CIRCUMSTANCES it would be best if you went home," said Kate. "Are you able to drive?"

"Yes." I went to hand her back the copy of the letter, but she indicated that it was mine to keep. "I'm fine. Classes tomorrow?" I knew I knew this, it had been a recent announcement, but I couldn't remember. What was I going to tell Tom? How would I ever face you?

"The school will be open tomorrow but no classes. I don't want to see you here tomorrow or the next day. We'll get Helen Gauss in for you."

"She tells them wild stories all day. Nothing gets done."

"That should be the least of your worries."

"It's not like the boy walked through the school shooting people."

"Don't underestimate the impact of the trauma, Constance."

"I am not to blame for this."

"No one's saying you are."

"Then why do I feel accused of murder?"

"You're human. You want to protect them."

"And I know what you want to protect, Kate."

"Now you listen to me. The boy you treated unfairly yesterday took his own life. Whether or not there's a causal connection there, people – witnesses in your class – will assume one and tell their parents about it. Those children do not need to see you in these halls, not for the next few days. And so if there's one person I'm protecting it's you."

WHEN I GOT home after work I had two messages. One was from Tom saying that his presentation had been a success and that, "not to jinx it or anything," he could feel a deal coming. The other was from Afzal. He had something to ask me, nothing that should worry me. He said he had been thinking about me all day, since the moment we parted after our drive to school together. "I would rather not be separated from you," he said. I replayed his message, five? ten times? – I lost count.

In the empty house, mid-afternoon in a delicate light I associate with summer swims at dawn, with the dog watching quizzically from its bed on the kitchen couch, I stood thinking about next moves. The door was closed; I had locked it. My keys – car, house, classroom, my mother's house – dangled on their blue cord. I still had my coat on. All I could squeeze out of my brain were two expectant words. It was as if there were no pedestrian middle step. There was in my immediate world either a momentous Next Move or nothing. Nothing to allow me to remove my coat, make a cup of coffee, read the neglected newspaper, pet the dog, plan and execute a meal. The question, "How did I get here?" did little but feed the terrible stillness.

Just as the notion of giving Afzal a lift to work had jolted me out of paralysis earlier that day, I broke the tight collaring moment by picking up the phone and punching a number I knew by heart.

"Hi Darlene, it's Connie. I need to speak to Afzal Khan, if he's still there. Would you page him for me please? I appreciate it."

I wondered how many steps it would take him. Would he go to the math-department office, which was not far from his classroom, or would he hike all the way down to the staff room? I could wait. I didn't mind if he took the long route. I smiled thinking about him forgetting that there was a phone close by, having to walk the length of the building and communicate with me in the very public staff lounge with its funk of old coffee, its male teachers going to seed around the ridiculous Foosball table, the women in conspiratorial pairs and social threesomes, the photocopy machine big enough to sustain a small-press publisher. Let him walk a distance to get to me, I thought.

"Hello, this is Khan."

"Hi, it's Connie. You were trying to get me?"

"I do not think so."

"You called and left a message for me at home."

"Constance! Oh, yes. I am so sorry. I did not recognize your voice."

"Don't worry about it. Everything okay?"

"Yes, very much, thank you. I feel perhaps it is better that we speak this evening."

"Why? What can't you say now?"

"I will say that perhaps too many people will be hearing what I have to say to you." His voice dropped to a whisper with the last few words.

"Just say it."

"No. Please. I am not comfortable with that. May we please meet together? This evening?"

"I'll come to see you. Give me your apartment number."

He did, sounding immediately relieved. When he began to give directions to the building, I reminded him that I had been there that morning.

WHEN COLIN GOT home I was still sitting with my coat on at the kitchen table. My empty coffee mug was in front of me beside a stack of magazines, and on the stove the kettle, its whistle propped open, breathed, the burner beneath it set to a low heat. Our green-speckled metal coffee pot, the kind that movie cowboys use over a campfire, stood beside the kettle. The black plastic cone filter containing a used paper lining and dried coffee grounds balanced on top of the pot. My hands shook as I turned the pages of the glossy young-men's magazine that had come as an insert in the newspaper.

Colin had heard about the boy who had killed himself.

"Tragic," I said. Thinking that it would have taken more energy than I possessed to explain why indeed the death of James Lungren fit with modern twists the classical definition of dramatic tragedy, I said only that the boy had been one of my students and the school had closed to give everybody time to think about it.

"What's to think about? It's dumb to kill yourself."

"You'll get no disagreement from me there."

"So you got a day off. Sweet."

"Half a day. And no, not sweet, not at all. Homework?"

"No, actually. Nothing. I'm as shocked as you are."

"How are you and Bing doing on your project?"

"Fine. Same as last time you asked."

"Don't get flip with me, mister."

"Sorry."

"Jesus, Colin."

"I said I was sorry."

"I expect this sort of behaviour from your brother, not from you."

"You mean he gets to mouth off but I don't."

"I mean I don't need this right now. Any of it."

An unwavering baseline of urgency in my tone made him back off. Perhaps, I thought, he is beginning to be capable of empathy. I watched him open the cupboard, take out a stack of saltine crackers, smear each with peanut butter, pour a glass full of milk, sling his backpack over one shoulder, and carry the small glass and plate out of the kitchen.

"Colin."

"Yes?" he said, stopping without turning around.

"Please don't say anything about this to your dad or Pat."

"About what?"

"The boy who killed himself. Your father is preoccupied with his work. He doesn't need anything bringing him down. Okay?"

"Bringing him down?"

"Yes." Turn around. Show your face. You're supposed to be innocent, oblivious.

"Sure, no problem." He continued carefully down the hallway towards the front entrance and turned to go upstairs.

The door leading from the kitchen to the basement closed as if by an invisible hand. Footsteps receded. I opened the door and descended quickly. I didn't knock on Patrick's bedroom door before turning the handle and pushing. It opened the span of a hand before stopping.

"Unlatch this. I want to talk to you." The light was on. I could see only a narrow band of the room, ceiling to floor, part of his desk, piled with clothes, books, papers, dishes. "How long have you been home?" When the furnace stopped running I heard the buzzing of music coming from his earphones. It was loud enough that he could probably hear nothing distinct in what I said. The urge flared in me to kick in the door or snip his rope latch with a pair of scissors. "Pat," I said loudly.

I'd turned to go back upstairs when I heard him open the door.

"What?"

"I said how long have you been – turn that off for a moment, please."

"I can hear you." He moved his head out of reach when I made a grab for his earphones.

"This has to stop."

"What does?"

"This. You, down here, going mouldy. It's not good for your breathing. How's your puffer, is it okay? Are you running out?"

"It's fine."

"Do you have homework? Are you even going to school?" I tried to look past him into the bedroom.

He moved aside, made an exaggerated gesture sweeping one arm: welcome, *entrez*, *madame*.

"There's nowhere to sit. You need another chair down here."

He picked up a jumble of clothes from off the desk chair and let them drop to the floor. Immediately I bent to retrieve them. I began folding them on the unmade bed.

"Don't." He put his hand on the top of the pile to prevent me from lifting a pair of his jeans.

"It's nothing. Let me do this. You don't even have room for a dresser. I don't know what your father was thinking when he built this. No room for the barest necessity. You have a perfectly good bedroom upstairs." I grabbed a shirt, which he snatched from my hand.

"I'll do it." His voice was devoid of emotion.

"Why can't you...?"

"What exactly do you want?"

"I want...your father and I want you to resume living with us, upstairs, normally."

"Like a real family."

"That's right. With your brother, who loves and misses you. With the dog. With your friends coming over the way they used to. With you using the front door and the back door as the rest of us do. With you doing whatever you want to be doing but in plain sight. Is that too much to ask?"

"Yes."

"But why? It's unfathomable."

He mouthed the word slowly and silently, then said, "'Full fathom five my father lies'."

"Excuse me?"

He turned up his music. He began to nod his head, slightly, rhythmically. I might not have been there, I was so quickly dropped from his attention.

"I don't know you anymore. You've turned into someone I wouldn't want to know if I saw you on the street. You've become rude and brutish and slovenly. A lout. How does that make you feel?" He pursed his lips slightly and narrowed his eyes, but the head-bob continued and his focus remained a spot on the wall behind me and above my head. His arms hung loosely at his sides and his hands made twitchy motions vaguely recognizable as air-guitar. "Answer me. You heard what I said. What has made you act with such contempt towards me?"

He shrugged. "You tell me."

"You're ripping out my heart. I don't believe that you are without compassion. I am trying to understand you and you won't do anything to help."

"I'm sorry?"

"You are a cruel, stupid, insensitive boy. I would say that you dishonour me, but the meaning is probably lost on you."

"Are we done here?"

"Yes, Patrick, I would say we are done."

"Okay. Good night, Mother. Sleep well, now."

MALIKA'S FLAT WAS never empty. Cousins, friends, colleagues from the small collegiate where Afzal used to teach, were forever dropping in, staying a few days, cooking huge meals, helping with his legal and business affairs, getting in each other's way, making things better and worse, holding silence at bay. Once when I expressed the desire to be alone, saying that I craved quiet, everyone looked at me with curiosity. They had heard about people like this but had never met one. Were all Americans like me?

"Canadian. No, we're as varied as you."

Afzal's nephew, Awais, was particularly curious and the friendliest of the regular visitors. He was a scholarship student at Aitchison. His English was fluid, inventive, and, beyond the confines of the old school, peppered with the latest American hip-hop slang. I knew nobody his age back home more enamoured of Hollywood, American music, television and video, and electronic gadgets.

"My dream is to live in Santa Barbara," he said, closing his eyes and hugging himself. He has seen that gesture somewhere. He must have seen Sandra Dee or Doris Day say something equally gushy and hold herself like that in an old movie. It was a soft-sweater, ponytail, fallen-leaves, poodle-skirt, bobby-socks and pedal-pusher kind of rapture, about as sincere as a paste engagement ring and a paper hat. But I'd been that age once. I used to hug myself that way so that whatever dream I was having wouldn't evaporate. When had I grown scales? When did I become cracked and brittle, an elastic band left too long in a drawer? I thought that by casting off my old life and donning this one I was being necessarily impetuous, open, unguarded, exposed, able to grow.

This city, Lahore, staid in comparison to Karachi, is still a wonder and a caution, as my mother might have said. You don't dare be a young woman who acts contrary to the wishes of her father, for example. A boy makes clandestine love to a girl outside his social circle, and who gets punished? Why, *his* sister, gang-raped by the incensed relatives of the dishonoured girl! Talk is always full of this sort of sensational news, as long as it's something that has happened elsewhere. If it hits too close to home, if the event has a blood connection, however thin, it becomes the unacknowledged spectre in the room. But not mere talk, when talk is free. Yelling! I've never known such a din. Nothing ever gets decided. This one is to blame. No, that one! The girl deserved it, some argue, it's the way of reparation, atonement. She and her sisters should have kept a closer eye on their brother, exerted their moral influence. It is written. I used to look at them aghast. I would never understand, they said. I was a Westerner, an American, and this wasn't the way young Awais said the word. This was a barb at the end of a curse. They were wrong. I've come to understand.

TOM CAME HOME at five, an hour earlier than he usually did. He had bought an expensive bottle of wine and half a dozen long-stemmed yellow roses, the kind I adored, their edges burnt pink. The presentation, he said, had gone so well, so smoothly, so convincingly that he had had an out-of-body experience in the middle of it. All the work, the late nights, the agonizing over details, had been worth it. The client did not even make them wait the week they had been prepared to wait. The president of the company phoned them after lunch to say that she would be sending papers over to sign.

We ate at the dining room table, where Colin was allowed half a glass of wine in celebration of his father's achievement. I watched him sip tentatively from the glass and make a sour face, the briefest of grimaces, before trying a larger mouthful.

Even this act, that of my son tasting wine for the first time, was happening on the other side of a barrier. Tom sat opposite me at the oval table, Colin to my right and close enough that I could have reached over to ruffle his hair, and yet the possibility of an invisible force field standing between us was so great in my mind that I could only watch.

Tom talked about each of his colleagues who had participated in the pitch. His admiration for them had the quality of a sports coach lionizing his star players after a win. He wore his pleasure openly. I took more of the delicate pinot into my mouth. I accepted that Tom was also on the other side of the force field. It didn't prevent me from sharing his triumph. I could watch from my side and not get tangled up in his energy. When he looked at me, lustfully, hope-filled, I looked away. Let's just enjoy this, I thought. This moment before everything changes.

"Is Pat downstairs?" said Tom. "I think he should hear about this."

"Right now?"

"I'll bring him some supper."

"I think he already ate," said Colin.

Tom would not be dissuaded. He put vegetables and meat on a plate, ladled gravy over it, took a knife and fork from the cutlery drawer, and went down the stairs to the basement.

"Tom, maybe...don't force him to do anything. You can just leave it outside his door. I've done that before."

"I know," he said, looking up from the bottom of the stairs. "It's like he's Howard Hughes or The Man in the Iron Mask. This is nuts. He has to rejoin the living. Is he even going to school?"

He disappeared. I heard, "Hey! Knock-knock," and a rap on the bedroom door. "You in there? Unplug. Open sesame, buddy. Tell me how your day went."

I was meeting Afzal in thirty minutes. What would my husband say if he asked why I had to leave? It was none of his business. I'd tell him the truth. No, it was easier to make something up. I'd tell him about the accident. I'd say the police wanted to ask Afzal some questions about what he'd seen, since he was standing near the front of the bus. I could say that he'd asked me to be present because his English wasn't perfect. I could help him understand what he was being asked and to formulate clear answers, and since I'd been present also on the bus I'd have a good idea what Afzal was trying to say. That was it. I almost wanted Tom to ask.

Well, you see, it's this way, Tom, dear. Ever since the traffic accident I've been thinking obsessively about this man, someone I hardly know. I even went so far as to drive to his building this morning to give him a lift to school. Later in the day he phoned our house and left me a message. Don't go listening for it, silly, because I erased it.

I waited a few minutes before following Tom into the basement. Patrick had opened his door for his father. I assumed it had been done without duress, having heard no contentious voices, no explosive sounds of palms slapping solid matter, no crockery shattering or music blaring. When I looked in, Patrick was sitting cross-legged on his bed, and he was eating, carefully, with knife and fork. Tom massaged the boy's neck and shoulders with one hand as he sat on the side of the bed, his feet planted on the floor. Patrick's head hung down, his hair covering his face. As he chewed he sniffed loudly and tears fell into his food. Neither of them looked up at me. I stepped away from the doorway, moving backwards, hushed, the way you're supposed to if you meet a bear in the woods.

The signs on Colin's bedroom read, "Mistakes Were Made." "No Entry." "Danger. High Voltage." "This means you, Turd Blossom."

"Colin."

"What?" came his voice from the other side of the door.

"I have to go out for a bit."

"Okay."

"If your father asks, tell him I won't be long."

"Okay."

I'm going to meet another man. I'm going to run away with him.

Not now, Mom, I'm on a new level.

ONE DAY, WHEN we were visiting the Khans, I asked Rubina, one of Afzal's married sisters, what had happened to his wife. Afzal was out of earshot.

"He never told you? She had an affair with a younger man. When was that? It would be almost twenty years now."

"Afzal said she's no longer living."

"Ah, so he did tell you."

"Not how or why she died."

"Her brothers upheld their *ghairat*, as was their right under the circumstances."

"Their what?"

"*Ghariat*. Their honour."

"I don't understand."

"They took her life to address the dishonour she brought to her family." She said it in such a matter-of-fact way that I felt my stomach lurch. The brothers served jail sentences of eighteen months each for the killing. It was eighteen months too long, as far as Rubina was concerned.

"How did Afzal react? How did he feel about what happened?

"It was his wife. How do you think he felt? He has moved on, hasn't he?"

Don't look at me that way, I thought. I'm not part of this. I won't be. This is barbaric! Civilized beings do not act this way, certainly not with those they purportedly love. Or did love have a different definition here? Did it even exist? Not being able to talk to him about his loss only compounded my sense of being an alien in a world I would never understand. Why did he come back here? Why did I follow him? Surely he could have secured asylum elsewhere. This was his home. I didn't belong here. I never would.

Another of his cousins, a man who reminded me of a certain French actor who always played an unshaven cop, *un vrai mec*, visited Malika from time to time. He spoke little, and when he did it was with one or two other men, tough looking, hardened, not angry so much as determined and patiently grim. He would arrive without warning, stay a few days, and then be gone for weeks at a time. Afzal held bundles of cash for him. The rumour was that he smuggled guns into and heroin out of Afghanistan. The mysterious man never spoke to and hardly ever looked at me. Someone told me that the man knew where bin Laden was hiding, that he was an al-Qaeda operative. No, he's CIA, said another. Neither, argued a third. He's one of Musharraf's men. Top secret, under cover. They never said, "ISI," simply, "They."

Ever since the Americans established a presence here, the billions flowing into Pakistan have been like sweet rain after years of drought. A few people are getting rich. Communities are prospering. Business has bloomed. Roads, bridges, sewer systems have been repaired or newly built. Everyone knows where the money is coming from. It's meant to keep Zardari and the generals in line. It means the Marines have a supply line into Afghanistan. The dollar: Caesar's visage on a silver denarius. Everyone bites into it, closes their eyes, sighs one brief allowable sigh of thanks before sliding Obama and Mrs. Clinton back into their fools' full motley. It used to make me anxious. They saw little difference between my face, my mannerisms, my air of schoolroom authority, and that of the former president's wife.

"The First Lady? Pah! She looks drugged," said Rubina.

"Madame Tussaud is missing a display," said Jaswinder, another of Afzal's older sisters, looking over at me to gauge my reaction. I was still exotic enough to be an object of awe and curiosity, but familiarity was also producing waves of unpleasantness tinged with contempt. The women could tease me and be surprised when I complained. They began to make reference to Afzal's wife, usually as a non sequitur in the conversation, casting an ominous pall over my presence. Who are you, really, Mrs. Hardy? Why are you here? When are you leaving? It may have been my imagination, but this was the cruelty I read in their eyes.

THE BUZZER SYSTEM to open the front door wasn't working, neither was the intercom, and so Afzal was standing in the entrance waiting for me. Unlike the Leungs' building, his had no large potted plants in the foyer, no amply stuffed armchairs, no Abstract Expressionist reproductions reflected in the mirrored doors of the elevator. He directed me towards the stairs, explaining that the elevator, the door of which was a scratched, stained and dented steel that returned no distinct reflection, was unreliable. He lived on the eighth floor. "You do not mind?" he said after we'd already climbed to the fourth.

"Not at all. Good exercise," I said, puffing. The heels of his shoes were worn down on an inward slant. The dimly lit stairwell had not been cleaned in some time. I inhaled his tang of sweat and curry.

Though he lived alone, his apartment looked as if a large family had recently occupied it and vacated quickly. A large wooden table dominated a long rectangular space that, had it been decorated according to the architect's intentions, would have been divided into a dining area and a living room. Large cushions littered the floor, there being no chairs, aside from a couch in front of the sliding glass door leading to the balcony. The piece looked like something students in university towns leave by the curb in May. He'd inherited it with the apartment. The walls were bare. The bedroom contained a futon and more floor cushions and mats. His laptop, on loan from the school, lay beside his briefcase on the bed.

"So, why am I here? What couldn't you say to me on the telephone?"

"You drink tea?"

"That's what you couldn't ask me on the phone?"

"Please." He gestured that I should take off my coat and sit on one of the large cushions on the floor. The parquet flooring had heaved and was coming up in pieces around the base of the steam radiator. Water stains marred the ceiling. He was using the balcony as storage space, with large cardboard boxes and plastic containers piled high beside a bicycle and an outdoor patio set – table, chairs, folded umbrella – which, like the couch, looked to be something left behind by the previous tenant.

He brought out the tea, which he'd brewed strong and sweet, and a plate of confections. He explained what each one was and how it was made. They were of a sesame-seed base, he said, and when he was a child he would beg his mother to make them. He confessed that he had not made these; his mother had sent them from Lahore.

It was quiet in the room. Normally such a lack of background noise would have made me nervous. I took my cue from him, sipped when he did, picked sweets off the plate when he offered. Listening, I could discern our distinct breathing.

"Was there something you wanted, Afzal, or were you just lonely tonight?"

"You will take another sweet?"

"Thank you, no."

"Mrs. Hardy."

"Connie."

"Connie. Precisely."

He excused himself, went into the bedroom, came back and handed me a folded business-size letter. In a single terse paragraph the school board announced that his work visa had been revoked. He was expected to return to Pakistan immediately. Canada was deporting him, no reason given. He was being given one chance to appeal, at a hearing scheduled in the morning.

"Have you contacted your embassy?"

"I do not know anyone there."

"Know anyone? You just go and tell them your problem. You're a citizen."

I didn't understand how it worked, he said, how matters of this kind were handled. He would meet nothing but an impenetrable wall. The official would say to him, Come back tomorrow, I am busy, and the next day he would refuse to see Afzal or to return his telephone calls. He had no ally there. He was a man alone.

"No," I said, "you're not," and I reached for his hand.

MALIKA HAD HEARD about a healer in Rawalpindi, and so we made an excursion there in the hope that this charismatic, who employed a combination of snake venom and hypnotism in his treatment, could repair the damage done to Afzal's feet and ankles. I so wanted to see him walk unaided that any cure, no matter how farfetched, was worth a try. He resisted the idea, but didn't want to disappoint his mother. Several of the younger generation, Awais and his cousins, scoffed at the healer's claims. But in the end, Malika got her wish.

When we arrived we had to wait two days. The result of treatment, after the healer finally saw Afzal, was that he regained no more discernible feeling or strength in his feet than he had had before incarceration. The short-term effect was a bout of violent emesis and a brief high fever, but what surprised me most was that neither Afzal nor his mother expressed displeasure. He paid the mountebank his required fee (I paid), thanked him profusely, promised to tell others about him and his services, and, amazingly, apologized for vomiting on the quack's floor.

What Afzal needed was the meticulous attention of a nerve specialist. On the train back to Lahore I mentioned it again, though not as forcefully as before. He looked at me with the same forbearance with which he'd surrendered to his mother. His passport had been confiscated and not returned after he was released from jail. They weren't letting him out of the country, not soon, and such treatment cost more money than either of us had.

"Why don't you ask your cousin? He seems to find money growing in the fields."

"That would not interest him. In his eyes I have done my duty. I suffer conspicuously, I am an illustration of the corruption of this government, an administration propped up by the Americans and NATO. I do more to bring down this regime by hobbling along with my sticks to support me than I ever could walking naturally. I am beginning to think that he is right."

"It's right that you're going to be crippled the rest of your life?"

"Who am I to put words in the mouth of the Almighty?"

It was not a good moment, the resulting tears, my angry belittling words. I spoke to him the way I did to my sons when they'd been delinquent.

He was being used. I could see him changing daily, becoming harder to read, less communicative. The slightest provocation could make him angry. When I asked him about the stacks of money he was receiving from his cousin and from strangers I never saw again, he said it was going to help build a school and a new hospital in the north. As far as I know, neither structure has yet been erected.

AFZAL'S APPEAL HEARING was scheduled for eleven in the morning in a federal-government building a few kilometres west of Parliament Hill, in Tunney's Pasture, an area that continued to bear the spirit if not the physical sense of its bucolic name. I reported to the security guard on duty and told her that I was there to speak for a friend who was having his visa revoked. After giving Afzal's name and spelling it, I waited while the intimidating looking woman scanned her computer screen. Finally she found the case number and directed me to a room on the fifth floor.

It was ten fifty when I found the room where the hearing was supposed to take place. I opened the door, which had nothing to identify it other than its number. Inside was a waiting area much like the one in my dentist's office and a receptionist to whom I gave my name.

"Are you a lawyer?" the woman asked. She looked to be someone close to my age, but her hair and clothes more closely resembled my mother's.

"No, a friend. Mr. Khan asked me to sit in, mainly to help me with the language. Sorry. Me help him with the language."

"Urdu?"

"English. He can function fairly well day-to-day, but he wanted to be able to understand everything that was being said."

"The hearing will be conducted simultaneously in English and Urdu. He asked for a translator."

"Oh," I said, feeling at each step that I had been and still was flailing in the dark. "Well. That's interesting. I guess he wants me to speak to his character."

"Have you submitted a statement to that effect?"

"No, I haven't." I expected to hear next that my driver's license was no longer valid.

The receptionist told me to wait. She passed through a door behind her desk and shut it. I stifled a yawn. The room was warm, my eyes heavy. It had been a night with little sleep. The receptionist returned to say that I could sit in on the hearing and make a brief statement in support of Mr. Khan's case. I asked if there was anything I was not allowed to say.

"Don't say anything untrue," said the woman, without perceptible irony. She ushered me into the meeting room, which contained a long table with space for ten to twelve chairs. The officers, two women and a man, were seated on one side of the table. I sat opposite them. A stenographer sat at the far end of the table. The man announced the hearing open, the court reporter taking down his words on her little machine. The receptionist put her head back in to remind them that I was not the person under review. Mr. Khan had yet to arrive.

"We'll give him another five minutes," said the man grimly.

Again I explained that I was not a lawyer, social worker or newspaper reporter but a friend and colleague of the subject of the review. Who, by the way, is innocent. When would I get to tell them that?

Each seat had a microphone attached to the table in front of it and a set of headphones plugged into a console. Where was the translator, another room? Another building? Country?

The question was moot. Afzal failed to appear, and the meeting was adjourned before it could begin.

"What will happen to him? He takes buses everywhere. Maybe he got lost." Why didn't I pick him up, demand he ride with me?

"He'll be contacted," said one of the women, who looked owlish and daunting like the Clinton-era bureaucrat, Madeleine Albright, and who refused to answer any more of my questions: Does he get another chance? Will a lawyer be provided for him? If he's charged with a crime, shouldn't he be tried here first?

I felt like saying, "Contacted? Sure: collared, thrown in jail, put on a plane, gotten rid of. He's not a criminal!"

The committee members were gathering their files in preparation for leaving. Before they could stand, I said, "There's been a terrible mistake. Afzal is a good teacher. There should be a representative from the school board here, or the ministry of education. You should see him with his students."

"Why did you not make a deposition?" asked the man, who wore an exquisite blue-silk suit and sat with the bearing of an African king.

"I only learned about this hearing last night."

"We shouldn't be discussing this, Mr. Morriseau."

Oh, be quiet, Mother Owl, I thought. Does your head turn all the way around? Where did you get those earrings? The Dollar Store?

"We're sorry," said Ms. Albright. "We can't say anything further about this. Not without the respondent or his lawyer present."

"He'll get another hearing, of course," I said. No one answered. The owl blinked. Morriseau slid a sheaf of papers into a briefcase. The stenographer studied her nails. The receptionist guided me by the elbow out of the hearing room as if I were a dental patient still groggy from anaesthesia.

ON MY FIRST day back at work, it seemed that nothing out of the ordinary had happened. As many of my students as usual were absent. In one of my classes, Canadian history, a prep I never felt I did justice to, I heard a student say that she had had a substitute teacher in math.

"He was like, go ahead, do whatever, including stepping out of the room any time we wanted. There was nobody left after ten minutes." I knew that the girl was in Afzal's math class. It was not unusual for a teacher to be away from time to time. One of my favourite heads, a boyish old wit from Manchester, used to say that he expected every teacher in the English department to take not one but two days of sick leave a month. "How else can you expect to survive to fifty-five?" Sanity savers, he called them. We were not to use them for catching up on our marking, planning lessons or reading any book on the curriculum. We were to read for pleasure, preferably something trashy. That is, if we could find nothing better to do with our time. "I fully expect at least once in your career to see you caught on tape in a news segment about nude cross-country skiing or after-hours debauchery during Winterlude."

Knowing that Afzal had not appeared at his tribunal, I was worried that something had happened to him, something worse than his having taken the wrong bus. At the end of the day I went to the main office to ask Kate about him, but the principal was away at the board office. Her secretary told me that the substitute teacher was returning the next day.

"He's off sick then. Afzal is," I probed.

"I assume so."

"You might want to keep an eye on his sub tomorrow. Sounds like he's a bit lax."

"A bit! We practically had to call in a sheep dog to round up his students and herd them back to class."

"If something more serious were wrong, with Afzal I mean, would you know about it, Darlene?"

"You mean would I tell?"

"You're a veritable sphinx, Darlene." I wondered what she was thinking. I could well imagine. This was the second time in as many days that Darlene had seen or heard me express an interest in the man. I knew how rumours began. Change your hair and people start telling each other that you've left your husband.

I was on my way back up to my classroom when I heard Darlene call my name from down the hall. Someone was here to see me, she said. I could use Kate's office if she wanted.

"Who is it?"

Rather than call it out, Darlene stepped expertly on her spiky heels, quickly with strides limited by the scope of her tight dress, until she was within whispering distance. Boys, perfectly behaved, were known to act out in class for the chance to sit near Darlene in the outer office while waiting to be punished by the vice-principal.

"It's James Lungren's father again. He was here yesterday. He didn't call ahead for an appointment. He asked specifically for you."

"Shit. Double-plus shit."

"I could tell him something, but I think he's already seen you here."

"No. Tell him I'll be right there. I just have to, you know, shoot up."

I went into the staff washroom, where I waited until my heartbeat and my breathing were back close to normal. Ten years earlier, five – hell, a year before this and I'd have had somebody like you licking my boots. Didn't you know how much you were to blame? Don't you now? The secret was to sit, evidently listening, not responding except with the slightest of nods of the head, until the father or mother or legal guardian had said everything he or she had come in to say, that is, what had been carefully rehearsed. Knowing beforehand what vitriol was apt to be spewed, I'd learned how to sit, look attentive, making gestures suggesting sympathy, empathy, acceptance, contrition, all the while drifting weightless elsewhere.

"Rope-a-dope," said Tom after I told him about the strategy.

"Same to you."

"No, it's from Muhammed Ali, when he was fighting George Foreman or Ken Norton, I can't remember which. Ali lay back against the ropes of the ring for most of the early and middle rounds and let his opponent punch himself out until he was too tired to hold his arms up and then Ali took him down. That's what you do with these parents."

As much as the analogy made me cringe, it did seem to fit. People like you, Grant, they whaled away at me, at the school, the kid's other teachers, the principal, television, music, sex, drugs, sports, the Internet, anything that could be to blame for their child's woes. The time required for exhaustion varied according to the personality of the visitor, the severity of the perceived injustice, and the attendance record of the student. Finally I would speak. I would begin, not defensively, but by asking questions, ones covering aspects of the student's life, in and out of school, not touched upon during the prepared speech. Often the kid's problems became perfectly evident as soon as the adult spoke. The less they had to say, the more bewildered they were by everything: their child, the child's lack of achievement, their own role as a parent, the present, the future, the misuse of their tax dollars, the return on the investment in education, the quickly receding prize that is post-secondary education. I could almost predict with whom and when during the meeting the focus would shift from the child to the parent. Sometimes it began with, "Lord knows, you're just doing your job." Or, "I wouldn't change places with you, not for a million dollars." Or, "This all started long before he transferred to this school. Of all the schools he's been at, this is probably one of the better ones."

So leave me alone and hire a therapist, I wanted to say to them. I don't get paid enough to listen to you gripe about how your life has gone off the rails. You've been dropping your precious issue off with other caregivers his entire life, since before he could talk, and now you want answers? Now you want somebody held accountable? A decade and a half too late for that now, wouldn't you have to agree, Mrs. Jones?

But this moment I was without a strategy. You were coming at me with something I couldn't deflect. "My son killed himself in this building. He named you in his suicide note. You and I were supposed to meet to talk about the way he was treated in your class the previous day. He came home crying. He never wanted to go back to this school. Now he's dead and I demand satisfaction."

Not this time, Grant, I thought, opening the door of the washroom, slipping out into the now empty staff room, opening the door to the hallway, turning right instead of left and taking the nearest stairwell to the second floor. I'm sorry.

I have nothing constructive to say to you, sir. I have no idea what was going on in your son's head. Well, that's not completely true. I do have an inkling, from the note itself. Read it again. Look for the reference to "straight." Believe me, I'm an expert at teasing hidden meaning from texts. It's what we English teachers do. For example, take the name Peter Quint in the classic Henry James horror story, *The Turn of the Screw*? Significance? Oh, come now, Mr. Lungren, surely. No? Not a glimmer? First Epistle of Peter, Chapter 5. Quint, five? There, the light's going on now. Verse 8, to be precise. "Be sober, be vigilant: because your adversary the devil, as a roaring lion, walketh about, seeking whom he may devour." You feel like eating someone, don't you, Grant. Chewing up, spitting out. Still don't get the significance of the quotation? And the word is "quotation," not "quote," which is a verb. I suppose I must tell you. In the story, *The Turn of the Screw*, James investigates his theme of evil, and Peter Quint is referred to as a devil at least once. "Peter Quint, you devil!" You little devil. How often have we used that very phrase to chastise our own children, especially our sons? Roaring little lion cubs. Causing havoc in our lives. What's that? I'm impressed. Touché. I've been called worse.

Despite your vituperation, I sit defenceless before you. The English teacher. I open the text, shine a light to help your poor befuddled non-readers see. They really are blind. Walking around in a glazed-over, mp3-bubble world. They're copulating with anybody who will have them. They haven't the foggiest about romantic love. Their friends are more important to them than you are. They don't even know that they're allowed to love, fail, care, question, be selfless, idle, chaste. So don't. This is what I would have said to you. Don't come to my place of work, where I've been doing your job for you, trying to bolster the foundation of your child's personality, and accuse me of having any role whatsoever in your son's death. That is simply not in play here, sir. I will not, repeat, not be added to your agenda of reprisal.

I was a coward. I couldn't face you, and you were not the most appalling apparition I could be facing. Forgive me, I said to the air as I gathered the things I valued from off the top of my desk and from out of its drawers: photos of Tom and the boys, a clock set in a cowrie shell, my laptop, a box of CDs. From the filing cabinet I took a cell phone I'd confiscated years before. Perhaps, I thought, I'll recharge it and wait for it to ring. It would be like holding the seashell to my ear and waiting for music to emanate from it.

I took a back stairwell to the parking lot. I was not thinking beyond each step. Get to the car. Open the door. Get in. Ignition. Blast off. I didn't know that I was not going home until I was well beyond the street where we lived. At Smythe Road, I turned left and took the exit to Riverside Drive before Smythe traversed the Rideau River. Weary dusk dropped its sample-case in the vestibule incrementally later each day now. The sun was a pewter disk balanced on its edge on the horizon, off to my left. I could never be doing this in November. I had to know that tomorrow was going to be longer than today. As much time lay ahead of me as behind, time I would have to let devour me like a roaring lion, before I could retire with full pension. I was only halfway. Please, please, please say we're past halfway, Mom, my sons' high sweet voices would sing out, a litany of boredom on interminable road trips. Yeah, Mom, you have to promise us and say we're more than half-past. We're past half, boys. The days they are a-lengthening.

I turned the car into the drive leading to the entrance to Afzal's building. I wasn't going back, I just then realized. Not home, not back to the school, not to Bing's to pick up Colin, not to the science fair or swim meets or hockey practice. And yet I wasn't leaving. Had I been pressed to do so, I could have come up with a page full of convincing reasons why I should leave Tom, abandon my sons, break my employment contract without giving the required notice. It wasn't that I was quitting. It was simply that I was not going back. There was a difference, and I was the only one who could see it.

AT FIRST HE wouldn't let me in. What did he think he was going to do, hide in his sparsely furnished apartment forever? He told me to go away. He refused to talk to me.

"Open the door, Afzal. I can help you. If you go to the authorities, they'll hear your case. They'll give you another chance."

He said it was no use, and that he'd be arrested.

"You'll most certainly be arrested if you continue to act this way. Open the door. Don't make me shout like this."

I wasn't thinking about anything beyond my immediate need to see his face and assure him that everything broken could be mended. There had to be a reason they were sending him home. He opened the door and stepped back to let me in. Two suitcases and his briefcase stood on the floor in the entrance. I closed the door behind me, gently tilted his chin up so that he would look at me, reached a hand around the back of his neck and kissed him full on the lips. My stomach felt as if I were riding in a car that had suddenly dropped into and quickly out of a dip in the road. My head expanded and floated like a balloon. When I moaned gently and found his tongue, he responded, taking hold of me tightly. I took his hand and led him into the bedroom.

While we lay naked and entwined I asked if he had ever been married.

"Yes, I was."

"Was. You never talk about her. What happened?"

"She is dead. I do not wish to speak of her."

"No children?"

"No. Please, do not ask me anything more."
"All right. I'm sorry. No more prying."

WHEN I REACHED for the handle the door flew open, startling me. Tom filled the narrow vestibule, blocking passage. He let it be known that his silent partner, Grant Lungren, had called while I was out. You'd been leaving messages all over the place. You'd gone to the school to see me, but I'd already left. Tom wanted to know what in blazes was going on. He's away all of one day, his major backer's son is dead by suicide, and where the hell have I been? This was some awful way for him to find out.

I had no energy left to float a story. "You have to be patient with me, Tom," I told him. "You have to let me tell it from the beginning." I felt his eyes searing me as I hung up my coat.

I convinced him to sit. I told him that I'd been to Afzal's apartment and that Afzal needed me to speak on his behalf in an immigration matter. I recounted the details of the bus accident, Afzal's reaction to it, to seeing from so close a vantage the cars collide head-on, and my small gesture of comfort, all as if I were hearing someone relate dispassionately to the police what she had witnessed. Telling Tom about the coming tribunal meant telling him the reason why I was going to have free time enough the next day to attend it in support of my colleague. I knew I couldn't talk about James's death as if it were a newspaper report. I tried to put myself in the drama as if I were a character in a play. I put it all before him: the discussion of assigned questions, the boy's charade, and my decision to expose him and punish the class for his duplicity, admittedly not the wisest thing I've ever done.

I tried to make him see. I hadn't been myself. Maybe I was in shock from having seen the carnage, the poor dead woman. I'd envisioned myself in her place.

He was incredulous. I knew how much he liked your son. He wanted to know what I'd said to make James do that to himself. He accused me of never having liked you and of hating your role in launching his company. All untrue and I told him so. I praised your arrival on the scene, Grant. You were our salvation. Tom would still be driving that grimy white utility van and wearing a tool belt if you hadn't shown up. I began to cry, angry at myself for not being able to prevent the tears. I treated James exactly the way I would have treated any of my students. He refused to believe it. I see from your face that you're having the same difficulty. But you must. It's the truth.

I remember a point in the discussion, if something so unpleasant can be called that, when the mood turned irreparably ugly. If I was going on stress leave, Tom argued, if my principal had deemed it necessary I stay home from work, why was I using that time to go help another man in a completely unrelated matter? Afzal had no one else to call on, I said. Then why hadn't I called Tom at work? "You had your big pitch," I answered. "I didn't want anything to throw you off." Besides, what could he have done? Been involved, given support; I knew that before asking. I told him the world didn't stop turning when he wasn't there. Things happen, things that have nothing to do with us.

Then he said, "So what exactly are you doing for this camel jockey?"

It was as if time had stopped and Tom was frozen, perched on the lip of the couch, and I could walk around, incredulous, in the moment. Though he had been on the attack, he sat with his hands on his knees and his head lowered, glowering at the floor as if he were the one receiving punishment. He was angry and hurt but far from penitent. As I beheld him and wandered around in the instant that framed his hateful utterance, I thought, Here is the point at which I can save this, whatever *this* is. I can shut my mouth, turn and walk out of the room. Tomorrow he'll have lost his rage. He'll apologize, say that the shock of hearing about James made him say stupid hurtful things. We'll wake up, forgive each other, be reminded of his recent success, and begin to repair what's been broken. A big-hearted person would let that happen. A saint would.

Instead I said, "I'm going to give the man a hand-job under the table while he pleads with them to let him stay in this bleak, cold, uncaring country."

He told me to take the video camera and make copies. It didn't get any better after that. At some point he announced that after the biggest day of his life this was the celebration awaiting him at home. I didn't realize I'd screamed until I felt the rawness it left in my throat. I picked up an old cigarette lighter that had belonged to my parents. It sat in a heavy ornamental base of polished pink granite. I was rearing back to launch it at his head when I felt my arm being restrained from behind me and the projectile removed from my hand.

"Patrick," I managed to say after turning my head and shoulders. His father tried to say something reassuring and dismissive to explain my behaviour. I thought, Say something, Pat, you're not Boo Radley, for crying out loud. He saw you there. Your father saw you creeping up behind me and said nothing. You're both against me, the pair of you, I accused them. If this was the biggest day of your life, Mr. Hardy, then I should walk. And you should, too, Pat, before you too are reduced to a shrieking ghoul like the banshee before you. Flee while you can, Fleance. When the smoke has cleared, the throne will be yours and it will be safe to return.

Nobody was barring the door; that moment was long past. We were over. We were toxic spill, breached levee, isotope fallout, the glowing result of a radioactive union. Of course the boy acted like a horror-flick spook. What choice had we afforded him?

Grant, I'll tell you. You think the worst has passed and that nothing anybody can possibly say could make the situation worse. It was Patrick. Tom and I continued to talk around him and about him until he reminded us that he was standing right there, hearing every word, every barb. He said – it was like a large pane of glass shattering on the floor between us. He said that he was the part of his father I hated and Colin the part I loved. I stood there, dumb, astonished, waiting for the full sense of what he'd said to unpack itself. Then more. "When you talk to Colin it's like you're talking to a lover. When you talk to me it's like you resent the fact I'm even alive."

Tom lifted his arm towards our son. "Pat. She – that's the last thing your mother would want you to think. We can work this out. We have to. I won't let this happen. I won't let us stay broken."

He was right. It was the last thing I wanted my child to think. But I had let it happen, nevertheless. It made me a sorrowful wretch, it made me want to die. And I remember looking over at Tom, my hopeful, hopeless husband, and thinking, He really believes we can be rebuilt, the slated-for-renovation family.

IN THE MORNING we drove to the Pakistani High Commission, where we explained Afzal's predicament to the Chargé D'affaires on duty. The official put a call through to the Canadian Immigration and Refugee Board. After a long wait and many exchanges by telephone, he reported that the best they could offer, if Afzal agreed to surrender to Pakistani authorities when he got off the plane, was his choice of flights. He would have to leave within the next forty-eight hours or be arrested in Canada and immediately deported. This way, by choosing and purchasing his own ticket, he could avoid the stigma of official deportation and retain some dignity. Either way, said the man, who rubbed his hands together as if working cream into them and who smiled unctuously, he could not predict what kind of reception Afzal would have once back on native soil.

We returned to his apartment, where we spent another night together. In the morning we put his bags in my car and drove to my house. I knew that Tom and Colin would be out and Patrick more than likely asleep. Like a housebreaker I tiptoed upstairs, threw underwear, socks, jeans, shorts, sandals, some light tops, my hair dryer, toothbrush, toothpaste, shampoo, and deodorant into a suitcase. I put my passport in my purse, picked up the suitcase, went back downstairs, locked the door behind me, and returned to the spot where I'd parked out of sight of the house. I inhaled and let out my breath. Afzal took my right hand in his and squeezed.

At the airport I bought two one-way tickets to Lahore. The next flight to London, where we would have a twelve-hour layover, took off in forty-five minutes. We were lucky, said the attendant who checked our bags through. Any later and we'd have missed it. Afzal had just enough time to call Nabila and Saleem to let them know when we'd be arriving.

"We?"

"Yes," he explained, "I am travelling with a colleague, Mrs. Hardy. There has been some difficulty here. She is my sponsor. She has been good enough to purchase my airfare for me. I am deeply indebted –"

But why was I coming, too?

"I will explain everything. Meet us at the airport." He repeated the arrival date and time. "We must pass through Security now. I cannot talk. Goodbye."

IF I'M ALLOWED to beat my own drum, I'm becoming an indispensable cataloguer. I've also fallen in love with Bollywood movies. Though the nearby cinemas tend to show highly conservative films, everybody owns a DVD player, and they crowd around the TV to watch such stars as Meera dance and sing in daringly revealing outfits, and, scandalous wonder of wonders, actually kissing her leading men! In one sense the films are amateurish, plot poor, thinly disguised excuses to showcase the music and choreography. Isn't this what Ziegfeld and Busby Berkeley did back in the early days of Hollywood? I quickly abandoned my North American snobbishness and let myself be swept up in the breathless, exuberant, goofy, infectious rhythms of the entertainment. Everything follows the same pattern, moves in waves, and keeps passion banked high by holding consummation always at arm's length. Anticipation is all. It's the cinematic equivalent of a pulp-romance novel. The younger actresses, Aishwarya Rai and her ilk, especially those from India, wear clothing that would cause them to be arrested on the streets of Islamabad. At first I gaped at the hypocrisy of the chasm between the private and public realms. Afzal and the other men would ogle the televised image of a young woman who was soaked to the skin as she emerged from under a waterfall, and with equal fervour condemn a reporter for writing that the contestants in a beauty pageant were so beautiful that they would have made suitable brides for the Prophet.

"If I saw her in the street I would cut her throat with my own hands, my own knife," Afzal said. I tried to read his face. Was he joking? I didn't really know him. I would never know him. He had to say that in front of his friends and family. His faith demanded it. And yet I believe that giving voice to the thought brings the speaker that much closer to the act.

What did he really think of me, the adulteress? If my father had been alive and had believed in honour killings, would Afzal have opened the door to him? Or to my avenging husband?

SECRECY IN MALIKA'S house with its many occupants was impossible; all we could hope for was a modicum of privacy. The half smiles, the raised eyebrows in the morning when I stayed the night, the teasing, all had the feeling of qualified acceptance. For now, they seemed to be saying, I was family, though separate and temporary, someone to be accommodated with detachment. Not marriageable, even if I were to leave my husband. I was not someone to be taken at all seriously, despite Afzal's staunch, Kiplingesque devotion to me. Mrs. Hardy: take for occasional relief of sexual frustration. Treat as one would an exotic visitor to whom something ultimately dismissible is owed.

I knew what people thought of us together: Afzal and his "Amreekan" whore. Afzal and his martyred feet. He refused to consider corrective surgery. My savings gone, I couldn't have paid for him to have an operation even if he'd wanted it. I'd earned just enough from my library work to pay for a flight back to Ottawa, home, though no more home than Lahore was to me now. At one point I did have a ticket in hand, one-way, Lahore via Frankfurt and Gatwick to Pearson International. I cancelled it, turned it back into cash.

Afzal was becoming secretive in his dealings with men like his sandpaper-faced cousin. They would disappear for days and sometimes weeks at a time. When he returned he'd be distant or sharp with me. Suicide bombs were exploding with horrific regularity now: in an open-air market in Karachi, outside a police college in Islamabad, and even here, only blocks from where I worked. Scores were dead or maimed. I knew he was involved in some dark commerce. I vowed that I would not stay to see him die. He said dismissive, contradictory or hurtful things in answer to my questions and accusations. What was I going on about? It was none of my business. I didn't understand. I would never understand. I should concern myself with women's matters. If I didn't like the way the country was changing I should return to Canada.

Finally I made him see that I knew. I lashed out angrily, then clung to him, the fabric of his tunic bunched in my fists the way Judo fighters take hold of their opponents' robes. I was bereft, defenseless. He stood supported by his sticks, impassive in my wake. He had gradually given me up as one kicks an addiction, with false starts, self-revulsion for his need, and with a regret that almost took what remained of his dignity. As for me, I knew it would be more difficult to leave this man than it had been to leave my husband. This felt more real. I couldn't do it. He could offer me nothing now but an idea; I was his slain demon. He owed me his broken life. He had the pious look of a dead saint, a face of tinted marble, placid, impenetrable. I accepted this new reality and came to worship him in a sexless, self-abnegating way. It turned me into a species of nun. I became his acolyte. Yes, you're right. Accomplice is the more accurate term. I'll stop just short of self-incrimination and leave the details of my involvement to your imagination.

THE OTHER DAY I saw Awais off at the airport. He's flying to Los Angeles. Such a bright boy, he reminds me of Afzal. He's been accepted at Stanford. Palo Alto isn't Santa Barbara, but he couldn't be more excited. He says he wants to be a neuroeconomist, whatever that is.

My sons are well. Colin informs me that he is taller than his father now. Patrick emerged from self-imposed exile in the basement not long after I ran away with Afzal Khan. Go figure. He took a culinary arts program at Algonquin College and works as a chef in a Korean restaurant downtown in the Byward Market. He lives with his girlfriend Julie and her mother. Julie is a waitress at the same restaurant as Pat. They're saving up to buy a house. Tom is getting married again. She's someone he works with. She works for him, actually. I was prepared to despise her, but I hear she's lovely, exactly the right person for him. She's young and vivacious, she adores the boys and is smitten with Tom.

Apparently I had to get out of their way before they could become – what's the term? *fully actualized*? Much too clinical, but it fits. It doesn't hurt anymore to think this. Really. I can't speak for Tom.

Afzal? He is no longer with us. I mourn his passing as if I were his widow. He was killed the same day Osama bin Laden was assassinated. I wonder if my love had the slightest premonition of how he would die. It wasn't a car bomb or an IED, as we assumed it would be, or the gunfire of our liberators, but the most mundane, preventable traffic accident. He was crossing a busy road when one of his canes became lodged in a crack in the pavement. As he was trying to extricate it, he looked up and saw a woman standing on the other side. She raised her hand and called out to him, he thought in greeting, but it was to warn him of a speeding vehicle approaching. As he waved back, a boyish grin on his face, a crowded bus ran him down.

Who was it waving, trying to alert him? I think you know the answer.

He saved my life, though I failed to save his. He brought me here. I have to believe this has all happened for a reason. I will never forget his last expression: joy in recognition, and forgetfulness, however brief, of his place in this fractious world.

I'm reminded of the stepping stones people place in the streets during the heavy rains. After the monsoons, sweepers come in the heat to unclog the sewers and pour disinfectant into standing puddles. Cats, hunched over clots of boiled viscera the cooks toss to them, know not to drink there. When you drink, take three quick sips then rest, as it is written. I can hear him say that, gently instructive. I love the taste of sweet cool lemon water and scalding tea. Let the spice not taint the meat. In the heat, vertical stripes of lichen on the whitewashed houses turn grey; with the first rains they bloom green again. Everything happens cyclically, time both fluid and static, punctuated by rituals endlessly repeated. Each morning the cleaning women replace the water in the large bowls that the bed legs sit in, and still the tiny lizards get under the sheets.

The fresh-produce hawkers arriving at the door the same time every morning. The household suddenly immobile listening to re-runs of "The Life and Opinions of Talkeen Shah" on the radio. It's their *Coronation Street*. My mother lived for *Coronation Street*.

Loving Afzal Khan knocked me off my pins, as my father used to say. When I regained my balance nothing was the same. I caused no small amount of pain. All my old beliefs seem misshapen now. How does one begin to sort it out?

I would give anything to see my father again. I would kiss his high forehead, ruffle his thin, monastic fringe of hair, feed him sweet *badaami halva* and savoury *saag parathas*, and tell him everything that has happened since his departure from this difficult world. He was a math teacher like Afzal. He would probably tell me that a wondrous, unknowable mathematical pattern governs all human affairs. He'd say, Connie, my darling, the hardest substance dissolves and the worst crime is forgotten. Eventually we sleep and all that remains is a kind of pure music. The only name I can give such a heavenly sound is grace. That's what I would have called myself – Grace – but my mother had her mind set on the more puritan quality. A constant is a relative term, a placeholder of sorts, something we invent until a better idea comes along. Constancy. Is love constant? Renewable, certainly. Love pretends to an ideal, though it waxes and wanes. Sometimes I fear I've lived my life trying to fit the confines and demands of an impossible name. Let's do something about that, daughter, I can hear him say: I hereby decree that from this time forward you are freed from the shackles of your given name. No longer are you Constance.

What should I call myself, then, Abba-ji?

Whatever you want. I've always been partial to curves. How about Parabola?

You and your curves. No, I don't think I'm ready to be an equation and I don't feel I deserve a name like Grace. Not yet.

Hope. I always liked that actress, Hope Lange. She and John Cheever had a fling. I could be Hope.

The thing with feathers. Birds have remarkable eyesight. All the better to scan the horizon with, my dear, and be on the lookout for a handsome writer. Avoid the alcoholics, though.

It's good to know that Heaven hasn't made you silly, Father.

Last night I dreamt I was driving home and I turned on the radio. An old song by The Platters came on. The timing of it made me laugh. Oh yes, I was the great pretender. All my life I've felt I was an impostor waiting to be exposed. I read somewhere that over half the adult population feels that way. Is this what it means to be an adult, to live in the constant expectation that you're going to be found out?

And then I was young again, stepping out of an air conditioned movie theatre into the muggy warm summer night, with that strain and others from the soundtrack, those earnest, sappy, painfully apt harmonies running through my head, and the tears came gushing and they wouldn't stop and still they wouldn't stop. I couldn't see. I had to pull the car over to the curb to avoid crashing. I turned off the music and the ignition, and sat until the storm in me had passed. My body ached from it as if I'd been a crying baby shaken by a frustrated parent. Still I sat, tentative and wary but thankful, for long minutes as the traffic passed, the headlights washing in and through and past me. Thank you, I said in a kind of prayer, a whisper. Thank you. And I listed them, spoke their names, the recipients of my gratitude, and the roll went on and on: my family, colleagues, friends, even you, it's true. Students – I could remember my pupils' names, every one, many hundreds over the years, what they looked like and the colour of their eyes and where they had sat in the room. It was astounding, a feat I could never repeat. When there were no more names to say aloud, I started the car. During the drive home only one thought disturbed the perfect peace of my regenerated spirit: that I might never see or smell or touch this land again.

You've been a good audience, Grant. I hope you don't hate me anymore, or hate me less than before. Yes, it is quite a story. Nor is it over yet. Remarkable, isn't it? One minute it's bright outside, the next we're plunged into darkness. There, they are beginning to turn on. You see, it really is like a fairy world now, as I said it would be, the tiny celestial lights outlining the grand historic structures. Have I helped you at all in your grief, even the least bit? I'm glad.

When we're home? No, I'm sorry, Grant, that won't be possible. You see, for one thing, Pakistan is my home now. I have made my way across. I will never go back, not as long as this country is occupied by an unwanted invader. It has nothing to do with religion and everything to do with love. And you, I regret to say, will not be flying back to Canada, either, not until you've fulfilled your potential, that is. You must realize what a prized commodity you are. A man of your, shall we say, *substance* is much too valuable to us to let come and go as he pleases. These hardy gentlemen will see to your needs and make you comfortable. It would be so much easier if you would accompany them without making a scene. I knew you would understand.

Grant, one thing before you go. I want you to know that I believe James did not die in vain. What do I mean by that? I suppose it means I do think there's a grand plan in place for us all. You should know that I'm doing important work here. I'm continuing what Afzal began. For the first time in my life I feel passionate about something, call it my own peculiar concept of justice. The world needs adjustment, recalibration, if you will, and you and I have important roles to play to bring about that change. You don't see it now. No one expects you to. Someday I hope you will. In the meantime, please help us by doing everything that is asked of you. Your cooperation is greatly appreciated in this urgent matter, Mr. Lungren.

Acknowledgements

I learned about aspects of modern life in Pakistan from the following books: *The Dancing Girls of Lahore: Selling Love and Saving Dreams in Pakistan's Ancient Pleasure District* by Louise Brown (Fourth Estate, 2005); *Taboo! The Hidden Culture of a Red Light Area* by Fouzia Saeed (Oxford University Press, 2002); *Leaving Home: Towards a New Millennium*, a collection of English prose by Pakistani writers selected and edited by Muneeza Shamsie (Oxford University Press, 2001); *Pakistan: Eye of the Storm* by Owen Bennett Jones (Yale University Press, 2002); *Breaking the Curfew: A Political Journey Through Pakistan* by Emma Duncan (Colin Joseph, 1989); and *Season of the Rainbirds*, a novel by Nadeem Aslam (Andre Deutsch, 1993). The description of the cinema-billboard painter is based on a scene in the NFB documentary *Bollywood Bound* (2001). If my story contains errors of fact or custom concerning Pakistani culture, the fault is wholly mine.

This book exists in its present form thanks to the uncompromising vision of John Calabro, who knew it wasn't yet a novella, and Luciano Iacobelli, who kept sending me back until I'd made it one. Thanks to Allan Briesmaster, who caught many typographical, stylistic and logical errors. I am indebted also to those who read much earlier versions and suggested invaluable changes: Mark Sinnett, Valerie Compton, Steven Heighton, and Dean Cooke, who coaxed it through three drafts of a longer novel. My first reader and intended audience was Sharon Murphy, whose love and encouragement sustains me every day.

Other books by Richard Cumyn

The Limit of Delta Y Over Delta X
I Am Not Most Places
Viking Brides
The Obstacle Course
The View from Tamischeira
The Young in Their Country

Other Quattro Novellas

The Panic Button by Koom Kankesan
Shrinking Violets by Heidi Greco
Grace by Vanessa Smith
Break Me by Tom Reynolds
Retina Green by Reinhard Filter
Gaze by Keith Cadieux
Tobacco Wars by Paul Seesequasis
The Sea by Amela Marin
Real Gone by Jim Christy
A Gardener on the Moon by Carole Giangrande
Good Evening Central Laundromat by Jason Heroux
Of All the Ways To Die by Brenda Niskala
The Cousin by John Calabro
Harbour View by Binnie Brennan
The Extraordinary Event of Pia H. by Nicola Vulpe
A Pleasant Vertigo by Egidio Coccimiglio
Wit in Love by Sky Gilbert
The Adventures of Micah Mushmelon by Michael Wex
Room Tone by Gale Zoë Garnett